BOUGHT BY THE SHEIKH

THE SHEIKHS UNTAMED BRIDES

MOLLIE MATHEWS

Blue Orchid
PUBLISHING

BOUGHT BY THE SHEIKH

THE SHEIKHS UNTAMED BRIDES

MOLLIE MATHEWS

ABOUT THIS BOOK

Sometimes, love wins. Is this one of those times?

Charismatic playboy Sheikh Prince Fazza na Hassir faces a challenge that will test his business acumen and his heart. When his life collides with Grace Hunt, a fiercely independent and brilliant CEO who has relocated to Aibud to escape her toxic family, Fazza attempts to win her over with his wealth and power.

Grace remains steadfast in her determination not to be bought by the sheikh. Their clash of wills sets the stage for a mesmerizing tale of love, passion, and destiny.

Set against the backdrop of opulent Arabian palaces and the thrilling world of luxury cars, "Bought By The Sheikh" takes you on a journey where love knows no boundaries—a story of two souls, seemingly worlds apart, who find solace and strength in each other.

Defying the odds and rewriting their destinies, "Bought By The Sheikh" teaches us that sometimes, unconditional love is the greatest freedom of all.

Readers who love sheikdom stories will love this one with its familiar enemies to lovers; opposites attract the wrong side of the track and forced proximity tropes.

PRAISE FOR BOUGHT BY THE SHEIKH

"I really enjoyed everything about this book. You think Fazza is one way by the way he acts, you can tell he is hiding a hurt, wanting to be loved at all costs. Grace endured so much with her family that she feared if she were to let someone in, it would end in heartbreak. I was so immersed in their lives."
~ Loreli

"Great story and world-building. I had never read a Sheikh book before, so it left me wanting to know more about Grace and Fazza's story."

"Readers who love sheikdom stories will love this one with its familiar trope."

"I think it's fair to say that our sheikh is arrogance personified, so I was keen to see how Grace was going to handle someone like him. I like that there's a lot going on."

Bought By The Sheikh is a great Billionaire story/series. I'd be keen to read Anwar and Lucy's story, too!

"The descriptions are exquisite. The author is talented at setting a scene and making the reader feel like they are there."

CHAPTER ONE

My whole life is a lie.

Grace Hunt fought back tears as she watched the video testimonial clients had posted on YouTube. The words slid over her like a contaminated oil slick on the pristine waters of the Arabian Sea as she listened to the praise they lavished upon her. "Grace is a wonderful person." "Grace has changed our lives."

The testimonials should fuel her, but now, thanks to the damage her toxic family had wrought, she felt dead to kindness. How could she believe anything anyone said anymore?

How could her family have betrayed her so brutally? How could her mother have said such shockingly unkind things when she was alive? How could her brother and sister have stolen her inheritance when she had been so good and kind and loving to them? Why had she become the scapegoat for her family's dysfunction?

Jealousy.

Wasn't that what the therapist, Issy Riley, had said? "They're jealous. No," Issy had corrected. "They're envious. Envy seeks to destroy."

"Families are meant to love," Grace had protested—naïvely, as it turned out.

"Sometimes there's nothing worse than family," the therapist had said.

Grace shut the laptop and walked to the panoramic windows of her penthouse apartment overlooking the glittering skyscrapers of Aibud. Tears fell down her cheeks. A month ago, she had had a loving family. At least, she had convinced herself she did. Now that she had ousted their lies, there was no going back. She had been a sister, a daughter, an aunt, and a cousin. But now she had no one. She was alone. Again.

Indefinitely.

After the scandal erupted, there had been no other option but to walk away. Fly away, she corrected, gazing out at the Arabian landscape that months ago had been so foreign to her. Was she destined always to be an outsider, she wondered? An imposter? A stranger? Even to those she loved?

She wasn't an envious person. She wanted the best for everyone. But in the end, it didn't matter. She was the sacrificial lamb in their ravenous hunger for slaughter. It didn't have to be like this, she mused. But after discovering they had hidden the truth from her last Christmas, she had no choice but to confront the facts.

They hated her. Hated her beauty. Hated her popularity. Hated her goodness. Hated the success she had worked so bloody hard to achieve. She was a modern-day Cinderella, living a nightmare. Except no prince was riding to her rescue. No handsome Middle-Eastern ruler to kiss away her tears. No desert warrior ready to battle her assailants.

No one to hold her.

A salty tear trickled down her lips. She wiped it away and

vowed it would be her last. She needed no one. She would devote the rest of her life to the one thing she could trust.

Self-reliance.

She would devote the rest of her life to two things she could trust, she corrected.

Self-reliance and work.

CHAPTER TWO

The next day, Grace Hunt sat alone in her lavish office, her heart heavy with a mix of determination and longing. As Chairwoman of Aibud Ferrari, she was used to making tough decisions and commanding respect, but deep inside, a part of her yearned for something more.

Her office, a sprawling oasis of refined taste, was a testament to Grace's impeccable style and her love for all things lavish. Every detail had been carefully curated to create an environment that exuded sophistication and power. Her eyes were drawn to the shimmering crystal chandelier that hung from the ceiling, casting a soft, ethereal glow over the room.

The walls, adorned with rich, velvety wallpaper in deep shades of burgundy and gold, nodded to Grace's love for classic elegance. The room was filled with antique furniture, each piece meticulously chosen to complement the overall aesthetic.

She trailed her manicured fingers over the large, polished mahogany desk, commanding attention in the center of the room. Its surface was adorned with an array of exquisite stationery and a golden nameplate that proudly displayed Grace's name and title.

Behind the desk, a wall of floor-to-ceiling windows offered a breathtaking view of Aibud's city skyline. The windows were draped in sumptuous silk curtains, their deep crimson hue adding a touch of drama to the already breathtaking vista. On either side of the windows, towering bookshelves showcased a collection of leather-bound volumes, a testament to Grace's love for literature and her thirst for knowledge.

She had come a long way, she reflected as she studied her surroundings, which transported her into a world where luxury and elegance reigned supreme.

Her thoughts drifted back to her painful past, to the relentless abuse inflicted upon her by her narcissistic mother and siblings. They had torn her down, belittled her every accomplishment, and shattered her self-worth. Grace had endured years of emotional torment, her spirit nearly broken.

But it was her father's constant criticism that cut the deepest. His words had echoed in her mind long after he had passed away, reminding her that she was second-class, a girl who would never be good enough. He had instilled in her a fear of failure, a fear that crippled her ambitions and left her doubting her own abilities.

As she sat there, surrounded by opulence, Grace's gaze fell upon a photograph of a radiant mother cradling her child with unconditional love. It was a sight that stirred a deep longing within her, one that she had suppressed for far too long. She yearned to experience the joy of motherhood, to create a loving family of her own.

But Grace was acutely aware of the dark cloud that hung over her desires. The cycle of abuse that had plagued her own childhood was a specter she couldn't ignore. She feared that if she were to have children, she would unknowingly perpetuate the pain and suffering she had endured, so she stuffed the desire of motherhood firmly down.

And then there was *him*. The man she would not dignify with a name. The man who had nearly destroyed her. The man she would never speak of again.

Determined to break free from the chains of her past and channel her energies into something constructive, Grace founded the Frida Foundation, an organization dedicated to empowering oppressed women who aspired to drive. It was her way of giving back, of ensuring that other women wouldn't have to endure the same struggles she had faced.

The foundation, named after the indomitable Frida Kahlo, aimed to provide opportunities for these women, teaching them to drive and giving them the tools to reclaim their independence. It was a cause close to Grace's heart, a way for her to channel her longing for love and motherhood into something meaningful and transformative.

But as she poured her heart and soul into the foundation, a part of her couldn't help but feel a pang of emptiness. The desire to have children of her own tugged at her, reminding her of the love and connection she longed for. She wondered if she could ever find a way to reconcile her conflicting desires.

Grace knew that her journey towards healing was far from over. She still carried the scars of her past, and the fear of perpetuating the cycle of abuse weighed heavily on her. But she was determined to rise above her pain, to create a brighter future for herself and for the women she sought to empower.

She glanced at her watch. It was nearly 6 pm and she had been invited to attend the opening of an exhibition by Lucy Ford, an innovative contemporary artist and former New

Yorker like herself, with the distinction of having married into Arabian royalty.

As she prepared to leave her office, Grace made a silent vow to herself. She would continue to fight for the oppressed women of the Frida Foundation, offering them a chance to reclaim their lives. Perhaps, in the process, she would find a way to heal and discover the path that would lead her to the family she secretly longed for.

CHAPTER THREE

The vibrant streets of Aibud buzzed with excitement as the sun descended, casting a warm golden glow upon the bustling metropolis. The air was alive with bubbles of joy as wealthy art collectors and enthusiasts, fully sated after immersing themselves in the world of creativity, prepared to leave the art exhibition.

As the crowd swelled around the entrance, a collective gasp rippled through the groups of people, drawing their attention to the arrival of an extraordinary spectacle. The hum of anticipation grew louder as a sleek, gleaming gold Lamborghini, adorned with intricate Arabic designs and polished to perfection, effortlessly maneuvered through the city streets.

The crowd parted, their gazes fixated on the opulence before them. The Lamborghini, a symbol of wealth and power, seemed to radiate its own gravitational force, capturing the attention of everyone within its vicinity. The car's gilded exterior reflected the cityscape and caught the last rays of the sun, dazzling onlookers with its brilliance.

As the Lamborghini came to a graceful halt, the sleek

gull-wing doors lifted upwards, revealing a handsome young sheikh. The arrival of the elusive 31-year-old Prince Sheikh Fazza na Hassir had been anticipated. The jet-setting sheikh was renowned for traveling with his fleet of cars to different cities, collecting various lingerie models to keep him sated, and extraordinarily generous philanthropic activities, but was rarely seen on home soil. Every tabloid and gossip column had rumored his arrival, but no one had expected to see the playboy prince in person.

His tailored suit, meticulously fitted, accentuated his commanding presence as he stepped out, exuding an air of confidence and playful refinement. His blue, penetrating eyes surveyed the surroundings, capturing the curiosity of those who had gathered.

Whispers of admiration and awe swept through the crowd, a symphony of hushed voices marveling at the convergence of exquisite machinery and remarkable wealth. All eyes were drawn to this unexpected arrival, momentarily diverting attention from the grandeur of the paintings in the exhibition.

As the young sheikh approached the entrance, palpable energy coursed through the crowd. Cameras clicked, and flashes illuminated the air, capturing this magic moment, eager to immortalize the intersection of opulence and artistic expression. The allure of this golden apparition, juxtaposed against the backdrop of Aibud's creative hub, created a visual spectacle that was impossible to ignore.

The crowd, captivated by the golden Lamborghini's arrival, soon redirected their focus towards the gallery's entrance as the sheikh seamlessly transitioned from the realm of luxury cars to the realm of artistic exploration. A collective hush washed over the crowd as he paused to admire the painting entitled *Desert Dreams* at the entrance.

As the exhibition doors beckoned him inside, the crowd followed suit. Eager to discover what had captured his attention and who he was here to meet. The echoes of excitement reverberated through the gallery walls, blending with the city's vibrant energy. Art and wealth converged in a moment that would forever be etched in the memories of those fortunate enough to witness it.

"Anwar," Fazza said, throwing his arms around his older brother. "I hope I am on time."

"Late as always, but this time it was fated," Anwar said, gazing momentarily toward his new wife, artist Lucy Ford.

But it wasn't Lucy who captured Fazza's imagination. His sister-in-law's talent was undeniable, and her artwork attracted the city's elite. But amidst the flurry of colors and lively chatter, his eyes found something else entirely.

"Who is that gorgeous creature?" he stammered, nodding toward the woman at the center of the room, her long, flowing hair cascading down her back like a waterfall of ebony silk.

"Grace Hunt," Anwar replied. "I doubt your showoff Lamborghini will impress her."

"Women love it."

"Not this one."

Tall and noble, Fazza stood amidst the sea of high society, his eyes fixed on Grace. "What makes you so sure?" Fazza said petulantly.

"She's with the competition."

"How so?"

"Grace Hunt is Aibud's newly appointed Chairwoman of Ferrari."

"That is Grace Hunt?"

"You know her?"

"I know of her. Of course. I just—I hadn't expected her to

be so exquisite. She is the indomitable force driving that despot Sheikh Mohamut mad with her quest to give women in his kingdom the right to drive."

Fazza stared across the crowded gallery, noticing no one but the strikingly beautiful woman standing alone in front of one of Lucy's paintings. She turned, her glittering emerald eyes reflecting the colors of Lucy's painting she had been observing.

Anwar watched as his younger brother, unable to resist her magnetic pull, found himself drawn towards Grace. Fazza approached her with the confidence of a man accustomed to getting what he desired, but this time, his desire ran deeper than mere attraction, and Anwar knew it. He should do. Hadn't the same love at first sight set fire to Anwar's resolve to be a bachelor forever?

Fazza crossed the room, his heart pounding in his chest. The room seemed to blur around him, all the sounds fading into the background as he approached her. He cleared his throat, a hint of nervousness creeping into his usually composed demeanor.

"Good evening," he said, his voice a smooth baritone. "I couldn't help but notice you admiring the painting. *Ya Kalbi,*" he added, reading the description below the painting. *"My Heart."*

Grace turned to look at him, her eyes cool and detached. "It's a beautiful piece," she said, her gaze returning to the artwork.

Fazza's heart raced. "As beautiful as the woman admiring it," he said, hoping to charm her with his words.

But Grace did not respond as he had hoped. Nor should she, he censored, admiration growing. She was no filly, no pretty bauble selling herself in deference to men with vast wealth. No, Grace Hunt was more than that. Much more.

She was an accomplished businesswoman with a brilliant mind, a formidable opponent to those who sort only to control. Her determination to ensure that all women experienced the freedom and liberation of being able to drive, married his philanthropic activities focused on democracy, education, and anti-discrimination.

Grace Hunt was a woman unlike anyone he had met before, and there he was, behaving like a juvenile schoolboy. *What was wrong with him?*

She gave him a polite smile and a curt nod, but her attention remained on the painting. She was clearly no stranger to advances from men. She had clearly come to the gallery for the art, not for idle flirtation.

Fazza was taken aback. Women usually swooned at his words and fell for his charm. But Grace Hunt was different. Unless she lived under a mountain, she would know who he was—he was sure of that. But she was not impressed by his title or his wealth.

He watched as she signaled to the gallery owner that she would like to purchase the painting that captured her attention, her profile illuminated by the soft gallery lights. Her beauty was undeniable, but it was her spirit, her passion for beauty and art, that intrigued him. Other than her campaigning for women's rights, she was a mystery, a challenge, and that only made him fall harder for her, captivated by Grace Hunt's enigma.

With reckless determination, his mind was made up. *Grace would be his.* He knew it wasn't going to be easy. Winning Grace's heart would be a challenge unlike any he had faced before. But Fazza was a determined man. And he was ready to fight for his heart's desire.

"Let's go, Fazza," Anwar commanded, tugging his brother by the sleeve. "We're already late." He beckoned to

13

his wife, Lucy, who was chatting with the gallery owner. She smiled and glided to his side.

"Fazza's in trouble," Anwar confided.

Lucy arched her eyebrows as she followed his gaze. "The elusive Grace Hunt," she affirmed. "He doesn't stand a chance."

As Fazza climbed into the Lamborghini, he turned to look once more at the woman who had snubbed him. People surrounded her, and yet she looked so alone.

As Fazza fired up the Lamborghini's engine, he turned to his brother. "She is extraordinarily beautiful. But she looks so sad. Why?"

CHAPTER FOUR

Aibud, known for its luxury shopping, ultramodern architecture, and lively nightlife, perfectly suited Grace and her thirst for escape. No one could blame her for not wanting to return to New York, she mused as she looked around her penthouse apartment, skillfully blending her love of antiques with her passion for modern artworks by contemporary Islamic artists. Her eyes lingered over the painting she had purchased that night, *Ya Kalbi*.

Lucy Ford was a contemporary New York artist who now called the Middle East home. Her new home and love of Islamic architecture heavily influenced her latest collection. Marrying into the Royal Family had obviously fueled her creativity, Grace thought with admiration. She admired people who found true love in foreign places, avoiding worn cliches of Internet dating, short-term flings, and even shorter marriages.

Grace loved Lucy's new works and knew she had to purchase *Ya Kalbi* instantly. The English translation meant *My Heart*, but she preferred the romantic, lyrical feel of the words spoken in Arabic. It was love at first sight, she mused as her gaze traveled across her new acquisition.

As she savored the wash of emerald greens gliding across a sea of gold, an image of the audaciously opulent Lamborghini arriving at Lucy's exhibition and the green-eyed desert prince emerging from it flashed in her mind.

An unwelcome kick of desire rose within her, as it had then. The sheikh obviously needed to be educated on the superiority of Ferraris, she affirmed, bending her will toward the sole focus of her life.

Her career.

"What do you do when, your whole life, you've been told you're a failure?" She had asked her therapist before leaving New York.

"You succeed," Issy had replied. "Only you redefine success on your terms."

"How?"

"What does success mean to your hurtful family?"

"Stealing," Grace had said unhesitatingly. "Extracting money by any means. Thieving, even from those you love. Oh, and then there are the lies. Success means being an accomplished liar. Lying is a sport. Who could get what, from who, at any cost—and get away with it."

"So success meant sacrifice. And you were the sacrificial lamb."

"I wasn't selfish enough," Grace had said truthfully. "The irony was that my mother limited my potential by telling me that I was *too selfish, too in love with myself, too bigheaded.* That I needed to play small so my siblings could shine."

"Why would she treat you like that?"

"I have no idea. It's not like we're a royal dynasty whose lineage needed preserving."

"Gaslighting," the therapist said. "It's classic, covert, narcissistic manipulation."

Grace thought of these things the following evening as she stood poised on stage, prepared to unveil the newest, most pioneering, legendary Ferrari. The ballroom of the Aibud Hilton hummed with anticipation. The utterly original design had been kept top secret, and tonight, Enzo Ferrari's pioneering spirit of innovation would take center stage.

Amongst the audience she hoped would attend tonight was one man she had never succeeded in seducing. The elusive Playboy prince she had glimpsed at the opening of Lucy Ford's exhibition. *Sheikh Fazza na Hassir*. He was wedded exclusively to Lamborghini. What an incredible coup it would be to break them up and convert the royal ruler exclusively to Ferrari.

Has she erred and been too cool when he flirted so outrageously with her, pretending she didn't know who he was? Of course, she knew. But he couldn't know that. Not if she was to achieve the professional coup of her career. Besides last night had been a social event, one of the rare times she wasn't working. She never broke her cardinal rule of mixing business with pleasure.

Throughout her career, she cultivated relationships with the richest men in the world. Grace prided herself on her rare achievement of never sleeping with any of them during her rise to the top job. It wasn't through their lack of effort.

The same could not be said of Lamborghini's shameless marketing tactics, including lusty, surgically-enhanced blondes with fewer scruples than a bitch in heat.

She searched for her target, shielding her eyes from the bright spotlights illuminating the stage. Invited for the most exclusive revelation the supercar world had ever offered, only the wealthiest, most astute collectors were gathered. Had she succeeded? Would the royal prince Sheikh Fazza na Hassir come? His love of Lamborghinis was purportedly unshakeable, her intel had told her that, as was his voracious conquests of the women who sold them. What Fazza na Hassir wanted, Fazza got. He called the shots. *Always.*

She stood on the stage, fully aware that by adhering to the Middle East's almost monastic proprietary dress code, she was employing the most subtle, tantalizingly aphrodisiac tool she had at her disposal. The cream silk Lanvin dress clung to her Marilyn Monroe curves and clinched waist, falling to just above her calves, showcasing her narrow ankles. Rather than concealing her beauty, the high neckline majestically spotlighted her delicate face and statement lips, skilfully accented in a luscious shade of red for maximum impact. Grace had commissioned the bespoke color from pioneering lipstick designer Poppie Pac.

Her green eyes, she knew, smoked and smoldered even from a distance, with chic winged eyes creating a strong but feminine vibe. As she surveyed the crowd, she ran her hand over her sleek black hair, gently touching the long locks caught in a sophisticated knot at the nape of her neck.

Her whole look was artfully curated to give her the exotic look she knew drove men wild. She wouldn't sleep her way to sales, but she knew beauty that was hard to get was a winning strategy. Playboys, billionaires, and Sheikhs loved the rare, the desirable, the elusive—and the unattainable. It was a formula for success that she would not be breaking.

Her eyes fell upon Lucy Ford and her husband, the royal ruler Sheikh Anwar na Hassir, then sank disappointedly. The seat next to them was empty. While not a condition of Grace purchasing her painting at the exhibition's opening last night,

Lucy had promised to do her best to ensure her brother-in-law's attendance. Perhaps Sheikh Fazza had been delayed, she hoped, summoning more optimism than she felt. Had she misjudged his appetite for beautiful, elusive women when she had ignored him at the opening?

She had waged a bet with her boss and staked her reputation on her ability to force Fazza na Hassir's defection from Lamborghini. She took a slow, languid sip of sparkling water and stalled for time. Still, he did not appear. She couldn't delay any longer. She knew time equated with money in the agendas of those gathered. The hand of success or failure rose or fell on her punctuality.

"Your Royal Highness' and esteemed guests, thank you for your attendance tonight," she began. "Ferrari is pleased to announce the most innovative, audacious, and ground-breaking release in the history of supercars."

She nodded toward the side of the stage, silently directing that the floor-length silk curtains concealing the new design be drawn back. She kept her eyes on the audience, wanting to witness their reaction when they saw the Ferrari XTC888 GTB for the first time.

The look of astonished bewilderment was not what she was expecting. Her gut churned as she turned. She sucked in a deep, ragged breath. "What the f—"

The stage was empty.

The priceless Ferrari was gone!

CHAPTER FIVE

In her bustling office in Aibud, Grace Hunt was immersed in a flurry of calls trying to trace the Ferrari she believed stolen. The last thing she needed was a scandal of epic proportions, she mused as she slammed the phone down.

She had worked tirelessly to transform the company into a global powerhouse, and her dedication had paid off. Under her leadership, Ferrari had seen unprecedented success, becoming synonymous with luxury and performance and exclusiveness. And now this!

Grace's phone buzzed again, interrupting her concentration. She picked it up, expecting another call from a member of her executive team. To her surprise, it was from an unknown number. No doubt the news had already reached distant shores, she mused, wondering if perhaps the infamy of her horrendous moment might change her life. What she didn't know was if it would be for better or for worse. It wasn't lost on her that the theft of the Mona Lisa from the Louvre skyrocketed the painting's fortunes.

"Grace Hunt," she said, forcing her voice to exude confidence.

"Good day, Ms. Hunt. This is Prince Fazza na Hassir. I am calling to inquire about purchasing Ferrari."

Grace's eyebrows raised in surprise. The elusive prince was calling her! It was so easy. *Too easy*, she thought with concern. Why decide to purchase a Ferrari now of all days?

"Of course, Your Highness," she said, forcing her voice to a nonchalant crawl. "We can certainly assist you with that. May I ask which model you are interested in?"

"Actually, Ms. Hunt, I want to acquire the entire company. I believe our collaboration could be mutually beneficial."

Grace's eyes widened in shock. She had never expected such a proposition. "Your Highness, I am honored by your interest, but Ferrari is not for sale."

The prince laughed with arrogant amusement. "In my experience, everything can be bought, Ms. Hunt."

Annoyance lapped her heart, lacing with awareness. She hesitated, wondering how best to respond. She knew the company's future fortunes were precarious. Global warming concerns had become radicalized, new buyers were increasingly demanding planet-conscious cars, and many of Ferrari's traditional markets had been compromised during the economic downturn following the Pandemic.

Only her business savvy had kept Ferrari afloat. She knew Ferrari's future success relied on continuous innovation, expansion, and investment. Perhaps a partnership with someone as influential and wealthy as Prince Fazza and his family could be the key to unlocking new opportunities.

"I am open to discussing a potential collaboration, Your Highness. Let us meet in person to explore this opportunity further."

CHAPTER SIX

The following day, Grace found herself waiting for an Arabian Prince, standing outside the grandeur of the Ferrari headquarters.

"Looking for this?" Fazza asked, pulling the Ferrari XTC888 to a stop beside her.

"*You*?" Her emerald eyes flashed furiously. "*You stole my car*?"

"It is my car," he said, lazily stretching behind the wheel like a panther eyeing his prey. " I bought it. Get in." He grinned, savoring the look of indignation etched on her beautiful face as she reluctantly slid into the passenger seat.

"Did you buy the car or the company?" she challenged.

He adjusted his dark sunglasses, hiding the mysterious depths of his eyes, as he ignored her question and set his strong jaw in a determined line. This was going to be fun!

"Buckle up", he said as he snapped the locks and revved the engine. "I'm taking you on a ride you'll never forget."

Ferrari's Aibud headquarters, a gleaming monument to opulence, faded into the background as he pulled out of the driveway, the powerful engine purring like a contented beast.

Beside him, Grace Hunt, the raven-haired beauty with a heart as fiery as his new acquisition, sat rigid in her leather seat. Despite her mask of composure, he sensed her heart fluttering like a wild bird trapped in a cage, her eyes wide and apprehensive as she clutched the edge of her seat as he sped through the streets of Aibud.

Grace was a woman of the city, he affirmed, wondering how she would respond when eventually they ventured into the vast expanse of the desert. Intimidated, to say the least, he expected. But she had no choice. She had to journey with Fazza to his kingdom, to the unknown—their futures depended on it.

"What is your obsession with Ferrari?" he asked, breaking the uneasy silence with a topic he knew was close to her heart.

"I was drawn to the passion of Enzo Ferrari, forging his company, his brand, without any formal education despite the obstacles," she said, tightening the safety belt over her chest as he placed his foot flat on the accelerator. "I admired his willpower, tenacity, and commitment never to forgo beauty on the altar of profit."

It wasn't the answer he was expecting. Her response was considered, value-based and intelligent. Fazza nodded his approval. "These are qualities I, too, admire."

They were off to a good start. Grace might be a better fit for his purpose than he had realized, he thought impulsively.

They drove through the city, the towering skyscrapers a testament to Fazza's relentless ambition. The city was a vibrant blend of cultures where tradition and modernity walked hand in hand. Neon lights flickered, casting a surreal glow on the streets that buzzed with energy even as the day waned.

Fazza navigated through the streets with ease, his hands

steady on the wheel. He was silent, his mind focused on the road ahead.

"Have beautiful things always been important to you?"

Confusion danced in her exquisite green eyes as she glanced at him, thrown by his line of questioning.

"Growing up, my childhood was the opposite of beauty," she said. "I wanted to work for a company that valued what I did—passion, ambition and the courage to prove others wrong."

Again, she had surprised him. She was so interesting. So unlike other women. "Wrong?" Fazza probed.

"I was always told my brother was the superior child. The golden child. I wanted to show my parents that girls can do anything. I wanted to rise to the top of the company dominated by men," she said, defiance glittering in her eyes.

"Why Ferrari? Why not Lamborghini?"

"I told you. I liked the history. I identified with Enzo. He didn't come from a rich family. What he learned, he discovered on the job. Hard work, sweat, and tears—both those tasting of defeat and those smelling of success. I like self-made men, not those who inherit their wealth from Daddy."

"Ouch!" Fazza exclaimed.

She pressed her fingers to her lips as though wishing she could force back the truth in her words. Her flaming cheeks aroused his confession.

"It's true. My father was a wealthy man, a king, a titan. But rather than being a force for good, his power corrupted him. He was a brutal dictator."

And an even crueler father.

Fazza gripped the steering wheel and forced his fingers into the leather, "I had no desire to follow my father's path of war and terror."

"But you live off the spoils of his riches, and you don't have a problem with that?"

"Has anyone told you you're very aggressive?"

"I don't like falseness." Grace's eyes glittered with the truth of her words. "I say what I think."

"I like that in a woman," he purred.

"Women are not supposed to be frank. We're supposed to be diplomatic, which I call hypocrisy. Lying, really."

Fazza smiled. "I detest liars. We're going to get on magnificently."

"You still haven't answered me," Grace said. "Did you buy this car or the company?"

"I thought I made my intentions clear," Fazza replied.

"Which are?"

"I'd like to make love."

"*Honestly*!" She rolled her mesmerizing emerald eyes skyward and muttered an expletive under her breath that evaded him. Okay, so he wasn't subtle. But he was a prince. Subtlety wasn't a skill he needed.

"That's *not* going to happen."

"Do you always play so hard to get?"

"I'm not playing," she shot back. "*I'm working*. Stop evading my question. Have you bought this car, or are we on a test drive?"

"A test drive? What a charming idea," he said. "Yes, I would like to sample everything before I buy. Very much," His eyes trailed over her luscious curves. "I believe it is customary to look under the bonnet?"

Grace raked her fingers through her hair and exhaled an exasperated whoosh of air.

A prism of light bounced off the Richard Mille racing machine on his wrist. "What is it that you do?" she said, her gaze lingering with appreciation over the high-performance watch. "To afford all this," she said, waving her hand toward the priceless Ferrari's bonnet as she stared at the city lights.

"You're looking at it," he said, gesturing to the miles of skyscrapers blazing neon. "I build cities from sand."

"You're a property developer?"

"I prefer the title 'futurist,'" he said, registering her shocked approval. "A decade ago, I saw the potential of the barren wilderness. I predicted the demise of our oil reserves and the need to diversify to protect the planet. I knew I needed to provide a future for my people and bring them, kicking in some cases, toward the future."

He slowed the car to a stop and picked up his phone. "Aibud used to look like this," he said as he scrolled through images revealing the wasteland that was.

"Wow, I'm impressed," Grace said. "It's quite a change. Your vision was ambitious."

"It was not without its resistance. But nothing ventured, nothing attained. Which brings me to the terms of my purchase."

"I wondered how you managed to buy this car without me as your conduit. I was entrusted with the sale of the new model exclusively."

"But you are."

"Are what?"

"My exclusive conduit."

"I don't follow."

"I told your boss I would transfer my allegiance to Ferrari. To seal the deal, it was agreed that your name would be associated with my endorsement."

"But gosh, that's wonderful," Grace said.

"Yes," Fazza purred. "It is." He glanced into the rearview mirror and noticed the glint of satisfaction in his eyes as he turned the ignition. He accelerated dramatically and sped down the smooth, newly built highway leading away from the city.

As they drove further, the cityscape gave way to a barren landscape, the sand shifting with the wind under the setting sun. The desert was a kingdom in its own right, a kingdom that belonged to Fazza. It was harsh and unforgiving yet held a certain allure, a beauty in its raw, untamed nature.

"Why do I get the feeling there's a catch?" Grace said, turning and registering the metropolis fading into the distance.

"No catch," Fazza grinned. "Not unless you mean my success in procuring you."

"Procuring me? I don't follow."

"I bought you. You are the catch."

"Is this a joke?"

"I can assure you, in matters of marriage, I do not joke."

"Marriage?" she stammered.

"Marriage," he said emphatically.

"I'm not laughing."

Fazza remained stoically silent.

"No!" Grace said. "That's a firm no! Just in case you were asking."

"I'm not. But if I were, I think you'd find 'yes' is much more to your benefit."

"Are you threatening me?"

"No, absolutely not! A gentleman would never do that. I was educated at Cambridge. I think you'll find me a very cultured husband. Not a savage Bedouin who wishes to drag you into the desert and impregnate you against your will."

"Impregnate," she gasped with horror.

"You have something I want."

"You have the Ferrari XTC888 GTB. I have nothing else to give."

"Oh, but you do."

"Which is?"

"A womb."

She threw her head back and laughed. "You must be joking," she turned to him, her face blanching as the relentless purpose dancing in his eyes told a different story.

"I have it on good authority that your harem is full of wombs," she protested, throwing her hands back towards the city. "Impregnate one of your own."

"I want to join my brothers in their mission to merge the East and the West and bridge our cultures."

"That's very admirable," Grace said. "Go for gold. I hear you've got your pick of European supermodels. Impregnate one of them. Don't stop at one. Take 12, 20, 50! I don't care. I know monogamy isn't the norm here. And I'm okay with that. It's just not for me. Just like children aren't for me. Trust me. My family is rotten. They've corrupted my DNA. I'm never, ever having a child."

"I want someone with brains and beauty," he said. "You have that in spades. You're clever, strong, resilient. A survivor. Besides, I think you'll agree that I have paid highly for the rights to your womb."

"Rights!" she lobbed. "You have no rights."

"You're in my world now. Not America. I think you will find the rights are very much mine," Fazza said as the palace walls came into view.

There was no turning back, no way to escape. She would realize that soon enough, Fazza mused. He glanced at her as she stared straight ahead, her profile illuminated by the soft glow of the dashboard.

"Bought by the Sheikh," she threw at him. "It's a great title for a fantasy romance, some escapist read, but I'm not in the mood for fantasy," she said, facing him. "But I am in the mood for escape. So, if you'll excuse me, I've had enough of this game. You can drop me home now."

"Is that an invitation to join you in bed?"

"In your dreams." She placed her hand on the door handle. "Pullover. I want to get out now."

"That, *habiti*, is not possible."

CHAPTER SEVEN

"Perhaps, I have gone too far," Fazza said, turning toward Grace as the Ferrari pulled up to the palace gates.

"Perhaps? Is that some sort of concession? Some feeble admission of wrongdoing? You can't snatch women off the streets, no matter how royal your title is."

"I didn't snatch you. You came willingly."

"I was deceived."

"Were you? I told you what I had in mind."

"Yes, to purchase a Ferrari. Not me!"

"It is clear that we disagree."

She flung her arms across her chest. "That's putting it mildly."

"Let us agree on one thing—we have three days. Three days to work through our differences. Three days to negotiate. Three days to agree, disagree, or find some common ground. Or I shall withdraw my offer to purchase Ferrari— and with it, the considerable fortune that could save your beloved company. And you shall be free. As for what happens to Ferrari?" he splayed his hands in front of his chest. "That is up to fate."

"*Fate*!" Grace spluttered. "You have orchestrated every-thing. The theft of this Ferrari at the unveiling—and with it ensured my humiliation. The lucrative offer to transform the Ferrari fortune—and, with it, my professional honor. And now with my forced internment within your palace walls—my freedom. None of this is fate!"

Fate, he savored the thought. Fate had indeed brought them together. Why else had Anwar asked Fazza to pick him up from Lucy's art exhibition? The very exhibition the deli-ciously defiant Grace Hunt was also attending. And then there was the painting aptly entitled *Ya Kalbi*, My Heart, which Grace had admired and purchased.

The whispers of destiny echoed through the desert, wrap-ping around their souls as they sat in the Ferrari, drawing them closer with each passing moment.

The question was whether the fates decreed their attrac-tion would last a lifetime—or even survive the next three days. Fazza smiled at the irony. There was no doubt they were caught in a force field of attraction. He was as magneti-cally drawn to her as Grace was to him, even if she denied it.

Fazza was attracted to many women. He loved women. That was his problem. Loving women was like loving flow-ers. How could one possibly crown a favorite? But now, in one fated moment, everything had changed. Crown Grace he would. It was not just her beauty and her considerable brains, nor the altruistic, visionary passion that drove her to empower women by teaching them to drive. Nor was it her fearless, courageousness in defying convention by doing so.

He drummed his fingers on his clean-shaven chin as she swung her long, slender legs out of the Ferrari and gracefully stood on her feet. She was an exotic beauty, he thought, his heart kicking as the late sun shone upon her silken mane of glossy black hair.

A rare black orchid, he mused. The petals of the black orchid are smooth and glossy, reflecting light in a way that adds to its allure. The flower has a complex structure, with multiple layers of petals that create depth and texture. The black orchid emits a subtle, intoxicating fragrance that is both sweet and earthy, further adding to its captivating nature. Yes, Grace was all these things and more, much more.

Drawing a similarity to the pristine natural world still did not capture how exquisite she was. How could he, a mere mortal, create a rational and logical list of what made Grace so addictively attractive in a way he was powerless to resist? It was as troubling as it was liberating. Had he finally met his match, the one woman he wanted to marry?

"Well, I might as well make myself comfortable," she said, "If I am to be your reluctant guest during these—" she paused, her green eyes glittering defiantly, "*negotiations*."

She spat the word out as though silently saying, 'Go fuck yourself,' knowing as he did that the negotiations were rigged. Fazza would ensure that what he wanted he got, and he would, through his formidable will and stratospheric wealth, ensure the result returned achieved that.

"I do appreciate the nod to democracy," she said, her lips softening as she gently but firmly defied his absolute will.

Another tick in her favor. Grace Hunt was nobody's fool. It would be a mistake to underestimate her.

"These children you mentioned making," she said, facing him. "Should we make a start? Perhaps, you'd be kind enough to show me to my bedroom."

"Bedroom!" he laughed. "What a quaint idea. No, no, no, not a bedroom. Not for the mother of my children. I think you will find *al qasr al saghir,* The Little Palace, more amenable.

CHAPTER EIGHT

I t was like stepping into a fairytale, Grace mused as she
entered her suite within the palace. Her gaze fell upon
the luxurious Arabian bed fit for a princess in the
center of the room. A flowing canopy made of sheer, ethereal
silk, delicately embroidered with intricate floral patterns and
fine arabesque designs in soft pastel hues, cascaded over
the bed.

If she was in the mood for sex with a rich and powerful
sheikh, which she definitely was not, the intimate and
romantic ambiance would set the mood.

I will indulge his little prank, Grace decided. Fazza's
claim that he had bought her was medieval. As unlikely to be
true as seeing camels with pink wings fly across the moon.
The man was on a different planet. Of course he was. He was
a royal prince with unlimited wealth. Her boss was obviously
in on the prank. Clearly, it was some sort of initiation before
they talked about a possible acquisition. Well, stuff them and
their sexist antics. It would take two to play the mating game,
and one thing neither of them should do was underestimate
her. So they liked playing jokes, did they?

Despite her irritation, she smiled, savoring a delicious thought. The joke, they would quickly find, was on them. She couldn't remember the last time she had enjoyed a holiday, and certainly nowhere as opulent as the desert kingdom where she now found herself held captive.

Huh! She would show them, she vowed, drawing the silk curtain forward to envelop the bed and flopping on the sheets. She would take a well-earned break from the demands of her career and sample everything Sheikh Fazza had to offer—all at his expense. What was it he had said? Oh, yes, that's right, she recalled, kicking off her shoes as she replayed his words. He was taking her on a test drive.

Well, she would take Fazza on a test drive, too. She would look for the gift in her misfortune and treat Fazza's disruptive imposition on her time as an opportunity to sample everything before she brought him to his knees, begging to be free of her.

Her eyes filtered through the fine silk, relishing momentarily the privacy and a sense of seclusion fit for a princess, then trailed toward the palace. Who knows, perhaps she would enjoy looking under Sheikh Fazza's bonnet and experiencing the full throttle of the power he mistakenly believed he yielded over her.

Besides, she could relax now that the purchase had clearly been concluded, she mused, nestling back against the plump satin pillows propped up by velvet cushions, handcrafted with delicate beadwork and shimmering sequins that add a touch of glamour and elegance.

Her sales targets had been more than achieved. Her successful conversion of Sheikh Fazza from the opposition would forever be cemented within the hallowed halls of Ferrari.

In the meantime, she would indulge in healthy lashings of luxury. What danger was there in playing a harmless game of make-belief, she mused, fighting the thrill of excitement rico-cheting through her as Fazza reentered the room, clad in nothing but 'paint-on' gold speedos that left little to her imag-ination.

"Shouldn't you knock?" she said, bolting upright.

Her eyes widened in disbelief as his muscles rippled gold fire under the heat of the fading sun filtering through her window, accenting the swell of his honed biceps and powerful chest.

"You will join me for a swim?" he commanded, grinning to her chagrin as he registered her appreciable stare dropping and lingering on the most private part of him.

This was no ordinary near-naked man standing before her, but a desert warrior, a leader of men, a man not to be defied. But she would defy Sheikh Fazza. Her self-respect demanded it.

It was hot, unbearably hot. Grace would have loved nothing better than to plunge into the refreshing waters fringing his desert kingdom, but not in her push-up bra and lacy red G-string. Nope, no way, that was never going to happen. I'd rather die of heat, she muttered silently.

"I don't have my swimsuit," she said, "Obviously."

"Oh, but you do," Fazza said, gesturing left to a giant wardrobe the size of a football field adjoining the bedroom. "You'll find everything to size."

Her hands flew to her lips, covering her gaping mouth as her disbelieving eyes scanned the sea of haute couture, evening gowns, and floor-length delicate silk traditional Arabian dresses. She turned to him, fury flaming her face. "There must be a lifetime's worth of clothes here."

"Yes," he said simply. "A lifetime's."

Grace's stomach spiked with the realization that Fazza had planned her abduction for longer than three days.

She gulped. You mean to keep me here, don't you?"

"Yes, *habibti*. I do."

CHAPTER NINE

"You can't kidnap Grace Hunt and hold her against her will," Anwar told his younger brother.

"Why not? You stole Lucy. Besides, I bought her when I purchased that damned Ferrari. At least I paid for my wife."

Anwar's face blanched. "Wife? You mean Grace has agreed to marry you?"

"Not yet. But she will."

"You're deluded," Anwar said, affectionately ruffling his brother's hair.

"I prefer obsessed. Deluded is crazy. Obsessed is smitten."

"Either way, you're playing a dangerous game, Fazza."

"It worked out for you," Fazza shot back.

"Lucy was pregnant. It was different. She loved me. I offered her protection. I offered her legitimacy. I offered her love. What are you offering? What does Grace stand to gain?"

"Me!" Fazza smiled, pulling his torso erect and sweeping

his hands along his towering frame. "All of me. Women worldwide clamor to claim that conquest. I'm offering it on a gold platter to the beautiful, thoroughly belligerent woman. And I defected to Ferrari for her."

"You make it sound like you converted from Islam to Catholicism."

"Don't joke. I love my Lambourginis. But if converting to Ferrari is necessary to prove my love, she can't find fault."

"*Love?*"Anwar shook his head. "You have no idea."

"What?"

"How can you possibly love her? You barely know her. Besides, you make it sound like you did her a favor and made the ultimate sacrifice by abducting her and forcing her to be your captive bride."

"I know plenty about her. Grace has achieved the unachievable. She's convinced me it's time to grow up, settle down, and have a family. And I've converted to Ferrari. It's a huge accomplishment."

"You're forgetting something."

"What?"

"Grace's feelings."

"She'll come around."

"And if she doesn't?"

Fazza shrugged. "That's never going to happen."

"And what of our brother? Have you spoken to Tariq? Have you gained his permission?"

"He is my brother."

"He is the King. What he says goes."

"Not a problem. He married a Westerner. What's good enough for him is good enough for me."

"I wish I had your confidence," Anwar said. "So you've given your loyalty to Ferrari, now what?"

"I'm going to buy the company."

Anwar rolled his eyes. "You haven't thought it through, have you?"

"I have. She can't leave."

"Why not?"

"If the deal crashes, I'll offload the company and return all the cars."

"So you're threatening her?"

"Not yet."

"Fazza, I love you. You're my brother. But, sometimes, your impulsiveness worries me."

"I wasn't impulsive. I saw her. I wanted her. I bought her. That's not impulsive. That's considered. I want to make my children with her."

"And what does Grace want?"

"She's not speaking to me." He lowered his gaze to the floor. "She—"

"She's with Hamad!"

"Hamad!" Fazza exclaimed, his brow furrowing with dismay as he followed Anwar's finger, pointing toward their brother, parading with Grace on the white sand.

Thousands of diamantes sprinkled on her teeny-weeny bikini nearly blinded him. She looked happy, radiant—like a Hollywood siren. But why was she looking so delighted? With Hamad, of all people!

She was playing him at his own game, Fazza decided. That had to be the reason for her rapid improvement in mood. Grace might not be able to leave his kingdom, but she had taken Fazza literally when he told her she could do as she pleased.

Too literally.

"I can't be having this. Not with Hamad," Fazza said, his

chest knotting as he watched Grace and Hamad frolicking together in the Arabian Sea's sensual turquoise waters.

"Pretend you don't care," Anwar said as Grace glanced toward Fazza and smiled seductively.

"What?" Fazza gasped, sweeping his hand across his forehead. "But I do care. I care very much."

"That's the problem. Give her the silent, stoic treatment. Make her wonder why you've changed. You're coming on too strong. Get her worried something is wrong."

"Wrong?" he asked, pacing back and forth anxiously. "That would make me look weak. What I should be doing is dragging her out of the water and throwing her over my shoulders."

"Like an idiot caveman? That's never going to work. Women like Grace Hunt don't like being preyed upon."

"So why is she with him?" Fazza scowled as Hamad flexed his oiled muscles, and Grace squealed with delight.

"Back off," Anwar said, gripping his brother's shoulders as he faced off toward them. "You're showing your hand. Feign indifference."

"And just how do I do that?" he said bitterly.

"Wave."

Fazza's eyes popped. *Wave?*"

"And walk away."

Fazza regarded him dubiously. "A warrior does not walk away."

"This one does. Remember what we learned in martial arts. What is soft is strong."

"You've got to be kidding? Hamad's going to get my woman." Fazza tried and failed to repress the pounding thud of his heart at the thought of Grace succumbing to Hamad's overtures any longer.

"Trust me."

Fazza kicked the sand beneath his feet.

"You've had a lifetime of women throwing themselves at you. You were born with tits in your mouth. Women like Grace don't like spoiled, playboy princes like Hamad. Or you, for that matter. They want—" Anwar exhaled an exasperated sigh. "God, I don't know what they want. All I know is keeping your distance draws women closer."

Fazza's eyebrows arched. "Closer. I'd like that," he said, allowing his mind license to roam freely as he glanced toward Grace. He gave himself license to roam freely over her porcelain breasts, roam freely along her shapely thighs, roam freely down the line from her belly to the delicious sweet spot between her legs he yearned to climb inside.

"Wave!" Anwar urged, breaking the hypnotic trance. "Wave now! She's looking at you."

Fazza fluttered his jeweled fingers through the air. What was wrong with him? He was acting like a smitten schoolboy, and women had never had that effect on him.

"Not like that," Anwar said, mimicking his playful wave. "Like a ruler—a man who yields to no woman, a man who commands his subjects with his royal indifference."

Fazza frowned, searching his memory for a 'come hither' royal wave worthy of Grace Hunt. An image of Rainier III, Prince of Mónaco, came to mind. He had married the beautiful Hollywood siren Grace Kelly after a good deal of rational appraisal on both sides.

Fazza willed his emotions to cede control and held his hand in the air, flat palmed toward her, imperceptively shifting it from side to side with feigned indifference.

"Good, now walk."

"Walk where?"

43

"I don't care where. Anywhere. Just move away."

"How am I doing?" Fazza asked over his shoulder.

"Fantastic!" Anwar chuckled. "She looks shocked! You've got her right where you want her."

"Not yet," Fazza said. "I'll have her where I want her when she's in my bed."

CHAPTER TEN

"Fazza! Where are you going?" Grace asked, panting as she sprinted from the sea.

Fazza forced his gaze from the tiny rivulets of water coiling down her breasts and fixed his gaze on the golden domes of the palace. "To bed."

"What's wrong? It's only midday."

Fazza's loin kicked as he gazed into her face and registered the concern that pooled in her emerald eyes. The strategy was working! He wanted to break into a smile. Instead, he cast his eyes downward and allowed his broad shoulders to slump in resignation. "It's the heat. It's got to me."

The heat of being near you. The heat of seeing you with another man. The heat of wanting to rip off your bikini and possess you.

"I need to lie down."

"Let me go with you."

He was battling thousands of testosterone-laden cells, yelling, *Yes! Yes! Yes!* Fazza forced his voice to a whisper, "No. I'll be terrible company."

"I insist. I'd feel horrible if something happened to you, and I'd left you alone."

Alone was not something he was banking on, he mused with anticipation.

"You would?" he said, barely suppressing the urgent desire to possess her with a forced lilt of gratitude to his voice.

"I mean, you know—in a nursing capacity," she muttered as their eyes met.

Her blush pulsed through him. He stopped himself from confessing, 'I'd like you to nurse me. I'd like you to kiss me better. I'd like you to look after my *very*, *very* urgent needs.'

He swiped his hand through the sultry air, dismissing the servants scurrying to attend to him as he entered his bed chamber.

Grace placed one foot on the threshold of his inner sanctum, the other poised mid-air, ready to flee. Her brow furrowed as though wondering if she had been enticed into a trap only to be devoured in an escapable feast of seduction.

She was wise to be worried, Fazza conceded. He wanted to grab her and throw her upon the silk sheets. Instead, he forced his racing heart to slow. Fazza saw her eyes widen as he slowly approached the giant bed commanding the royal suite.

"I feel so faint," he whispered, gasping slightly.

Grace came to him as he knew she would and wrapped a tender arm around his side.

Skin upon skin! It was more than he could bear.

"I don't know what's come over me," he stammered. He did. Of course, he did! He raked his hands through his hair. God, it was agony. He wanted to plunge his hands down her bikini top and flop those majestic breasts in his hands, cup them in his fingers, and lower his mouth to those pert nipples. He wanted—

Stop! He censored silently. Stop before you show your true intent, and she flees from your lair.

"Do you want to lie down?" she whispered.

Only if you lie on me.

"You're shaking, Fazza. Do you have a fever?"

I'm on fire, he conceded inwardly. *I'm aching to make love to you.*

Delirious with urgent need, his gaze followed Grace as she went to the bathroom and returned with a damp cloth. She bent over him and wiped his brow. He closed his eyes as the soft mounds of her enticing breasts brushed his nose. His body convulsed with desire as he inhaled the sultry scent of frankincense and desert dreams and drew them deep into his nose.

It took Fazza's considerable willpower to stop himself from wrenching Grace on top of his chest and then flipping her beneath him, rendering her powerless to resist.

"I'm so cold," he lied.

"Will it help if I lie beside you?"

Would it help? Hell, yes!

"You've done enough," he whispered, summoning his most feeble, ragged breath. "Go back and enjoy your swim with Hamad."

"I couldn't possibly leave you," she said. "There. How's that?" Grace asked as she lay beside him, snuggling against his chest.

"Better," he rasped. Better was an understatement. She felt like heaven.

"And this?"

His eyes shot open as her hands slid under his shorts. *"What the—?"*

"I know you're faking your illness, Fazza. You're a terrible liar, which isn't a bad thing. But the body never lies," she said, cupping her finger around his very excited royal penis. "There's nothing fake about this."

His mouth gaped wide. Her eyes sparkled with mischief as she reveled in his shock.

Fazza lay frozen as Grace withdrew her hand and pressed her fingertips to his open lips. She inched closer, her scent enveloping him, rendering him powerless.

Grace was seducing him. But why? She hated him. *Didn't she?*

She reached for his hand with a confident yet gentle touch, entwining her fingers with his. Fazza felt a surge of electricity shoot through his body, his heart pounding in his chest.

Their eyes locked, and time dissolved in a veil of bliss. Her gaze held a silent invitation, a promise of something extraordinary. Fazza's breath caught in his throat as he realized he was about to experience a kiss like no other.

She leaned over him, her lips brushing against his in the softest caresses, consuming him in a sandstorm of emotions. Shocked surprise mingled with desire, and he surrendered to the power she wielded.

Fazza's mind went blank as he lost himself in her taste, his senses overwhelmed by the sweetness of her lips. Their tongues danced in a realm of their own, the desert kingdom and royal expectations fading into insignificance.

Grace's kiss was a revelation, a symphony of passion and tenderness. When they finally parted, Fazza's eyes fluttered open, his heart racing with a newfound desire. Grace had awakened something within him, a hunger for love that he had never known before. In that golden moment, Fazza realized that sometimes, the most extraordinary things happen when you cede control. They had connected in a way he hoped would forever change their lives.

"Grace," he drawled as the spell broke, and she slid from the sheets. Her graceful steps barely made a sound on the marble floor as she walked from the bed. "Good Grace, don't leave."

"You bought me, didn't you?" she tossed at him. "What else would his majesty like from his paid-for wife?"

She was trying to be fierce, but he sensed their kiss also threw her. Whatever game she was playing, he liked it, he conceded. *Very much.*

Rising from the bed, he strode toward her and swept her into his arms.

"You've made a remarkable recovery," she murmured, wrapping her slim legs around his waist.

"What can I say? You are an impeccable nurse."

"What is it you want, Fazza?" she whispered breathlessly.

"There is something," he said, walking toward the outdoor shower on the rooftop garden adjoining the royal suite. I'd like to see you—all of you—n*aked*."

CHAPTER ELEVEN

This was so wrong. She had taken things too far. But why had kissing Fazza felt so right?

She wriggled feebly in his arms. She should stop whatever had started. Now! She had broken her cardinal rule: never, ever mix business with pleasure.

Pleasure! When was the last time she had ever surrendered to pleasure, she realized with a jolt. Her competitors ate pleasure for breakfast. Lunch. And dinner. Why should she starve, she reasoned. Because you have rules, she censored.

She had meant to kiss him fiercely, summoning her alpha female. She had meant to kiss him angrily to show him she would never yield to his desire to rule over her. She had meant—

Hell! She didn't know what anything meant anymore. But she knew she had not meant to kiss him like a schoolgirl sweetheart with a massive man crush.

Curiosity took hold of her. What would happen if she allowed herself a tiny, weeny lick of pleasure? Perhaps she'd taken her vow of abstinence too far. All work and no play makes. . .

A workaholic without a love life.

Grace's mind raced with a mixture of resistance and desire as steam enveloped the opulent marble shower and coiled toward the desert sky.

Fazza stood tall and regal, his chiseled features accentuated by the water glistening on his olive skin as the warm water cascaded down their bodies.

Her heart pulsed as Fazza's strong hands gently cupped her face, his touch both commanding and tender. His blue eyes bore into hers, a silent promise of passion and intensity. The air crackled with an electric tension, pulling them closer, fate intertwining their destinies.

Their bodies drew magnetically toward each other. Grace's pulse quickened as Fazza slipped the straps of her bikini from her shoulders and undid the back clasp. As her top slid to the floor, his lips descended upon hers, a soft, lingering kiss that spoke volumes of their unspoken connection.

The water cascaded over her breasts as his powerful chest pressed to hers, amplifying the intensity of their embrace and heightening their senses as he drew her to him. Grace's fingers tangled in Fazza's ebony locks, pulling him closer as their kiss deepened. A symphony of desire echoed through every touch, every brush of their lips.

They lost themselves in the passionate dance, their bodies responding to the primal yearning that had been building since their first fleeting encounter. The shower became a sanctuary, a sacred space where they could explore the depths of their desire without constraints.

Grace tasted the exotic blend of Fazza's lips, a heady mix of power and vulnerability. In that moment, she let go of her rules never to mix business and pleasure, allowing herself to be consumed by the all-encompassing passion pulsating between them.

"Ya Kalbi," he murmured. The lilt of his voice repeating the name of the painting she had purchased the fateful night they had met vibrated through her.

"My heart," she whispered back. What was she saying? What had possessed her?

The water caressed their bodies, mimicking their writhing movements as they kissed with an intensity that defied the boundaries of their separate worlds. Days ago, she had feared she would never have anyone to hold, and now they found solace in each other's arms. But wait! Wasn't she supposed to be seducing the Sheikh? Making it clear that she may be powerless to prevent him from acquiring her company, but she could never be bought? Wasn't she meant to be making his life so difficult that he couldn't wait to be rid of her?

Flow, she affirmed as his kiss deepened. *Just flow*.

If there were a Guinness Book of Records for kissing, that would have been it, she thought as their lips finally parted. Fazza held Grace close, his forehead resting against hers, their breaths mingling in the steamy air.

Grace's heart raced with excitement and trepidation as she felt Fazza's firm contours against hers. His touch was electrifying, sending shivers down her spine and igniting a fire within her that nothing could quench.

The steamy shower became a sanctuary of uninhibited desire as Fazza and Grace embraced each other, their bodies pressed together in a fiery tango. The water cascading down their entwined forms only heightened the power of their connection.

Fazza's hands slid her bikini bottoms down her thighs. She stepped out of them and kicked them free. He roamed her naked body with a delicate urgency, exploring every curve and contour as if he were discovering a treasure. The sensation of his touch, combined with the warm water caressing their skin, overloaded her senses, taking her desire to new heights.

"*Ya Kalbi,*" she whispered as the water cascaded over them.

Their lips met again with a hunger that could not be contained. His kiss was fierce and demanding, a collision of passion and longing that threatened to consume them both. Their tongues danced in an intricate battle of desire, exploring every crevice and corner of each other's mouths.

Grace's hands gripped Fazza's muscular shoulders, her nails digging into his skin as she surrendered herself to the intoxicating pleasure of the moment. The prince, in turn, held her with an unyielding strength, his touch simultaneously possessive and gentle.

Their bodies moved in perfect synchronization, their desires melding into one. Their eyes locked, the unspoken promise of more lingering between them. In that moment, they both knew what they had experienced was not just a fleeting carnal infatuation but a waterfall of vulnerability and raw emotion. For a moment, energized by the sacred touch of water, two parched souls from different worlds found solace and connection.

But then, as Fazza reached for the taps and turned the shower off, Grace felt the magic that had held them spellbound disappear. She watched with naked awareness as the last water droplets trickled down the drain.

Nothing good ever lasts.

She wrenched free of Fazza's embrace. She stepped from the shower and reached for a silk robe. Wrapping it around her, she turned momentarily. Once they had been united, ready to face the challenges their forbidden love would undoubtedly bring, but she now saw only pain.

"We can't do this," she cried over her shoulder as she sprinted from the room.

"*This?*" he called after her.

"*This is not business.*"

CHAPTER TWELVE

Fazza stood under the steady stream of the shower, the hot water washing away the remnants of their passionate encounter. But as the steam surrounded him, so did a cloud of regret. His heart ached with the weight of the consequences their love could bring.

He couldn't help but replay the electrifying moments in his mind, the taste of Grace's lips and the feel of her body against his. The desire that had consumed him was undeniable, but so was the reality of their situation. What if the unthinkable happened and Tariq refused to consent to their marriage?

Fazza's hand pressed against the cold tiles, his mind filled with conflicting emotions. He knew that if his oldest brother withheld his permission, their love, even if Grace gave it, would be forbidden, and his family or kingdom could never accept their union. The weight of tradition and duty crushed his heart as he realized the pain their love could inflict on them.

He closed his eyes, his chest tightening with each breath.

The thought of Grace caught in the crossfire of their forbidden love tore at his soul.

As the water continued to pour over him, Fazza knew that he had to make a choice, even though it felt impossible. He couldn't bear to see Grace suffer but he couldn't deny their shared intense connection.

Regret washed over him like the water, weighing him down. He knew that he should have resisted the temptation that Grace presented. Anwar was right. He had behaved recklessly. But love, like water, finds its way through the tiniest cracks, and he couldn't fight the fact that Grace filled every crevice of his broken heart.

Fazza heaved a sigh, realizing the problematic path ahead settling within him. He knew that he would have to face Tariq and risk his family's disapproval and the challenges ahead when he told them he wanted to make his love for Grace official.

As he stepped out of the shower, he couldn't deny the flicker of hope still burning within him. Grace would be his wife—no matter what difficulty they faced.

Fazza wrapped a towel around his waist, his mind filled with thoughts of Grace. He knew their love was a dangerous dance, but it was a dance he couldn't resist. As he left the bathroom, the weight of his choices settled upon his shoulders, knowing that his next step would shape their destinies.

CHAPTER THIRTEEN

"Don't you think you're being hypocritical, Tariq? You married a Westerner. Anwar married a Westerner. Why not me?" Fazza asked his brother over coffee.

"I understand how you feel. I do," Tariq said. "But times have changed. Things are difficult."

"Things were difficult when you wed."

"Opposing forces are growing louder. People are questioning the place of commoners in The Royal Family We need a pure lineage."

"Pure! Show me a pure lineage. William, the British heir to the throne, married Kate, the daughter of a former air hostess. She's a commoner and much loved by her people. The Danish heir, now king after his mother abdicated, married an Australian woman he met in a bar. Who cares about purity?"

"The Fundamentalist State."

Anger burst through Fazza. "The FS? Fuck the FS. Since when have we cared a damn about the FS. What's this really about Tariq? Why can't you be happy for me?"

"I am. It's just—don't you think you're being a bit rash?

What's the hurry? Slow down. Get to know the woman you're so impatient to marry."

"Slow down? I'm 31. Do you want me to be an old man like our father, so fixed in his ways that he couldn't be bothered with us? A father bitter and broken by the betrayal of a wife who didn't want him? A father swatting away our desire for affection with the brutal indifference of a marauding elephant stomping on the heart of an ant. Who spoke to us only to tell us what irritants we were. Is that what you want?"

"You're being emotional, Fazza."

"I'm a Cancerian. Of course, I'm emotional. Grace is important to me. Anyhow, I don't need your approval. I will do what I feel is best."

"Let us not argue, Fazza."

"Let us agree, you mean. Let us agree that I will do your bidding and marry a woman of pedigree, a woman who holds the prerequisite DNA, a woman unpalatable to me. I don't love Shamira. I love Grace. Just because you are older by birth does not give you the right to rule over my fate."

"You would defy me?"

"No. I will ignore you. You're acting so strangely. You're not like yourself at all. Something else, *or someone else*, is bothering you. Something, *or someone,* you're not telling me. What secrets are you hiding, brother."

"You can't marry a divorcee."

Fazza's gut lurched. *Divorcee? Grace had been married? Why did he not know that?*

"Why not? King Charles did and defied his dead mother's wishes and crowned the divorcee Queen of England," Fazza said tersely, covering his shocked surprise at the revelation.

"It's not the same. Sheikh Mohamud—" Tariq began.

"That despot! He's so wrapped up in his bid for personal power he'll do anything to succeed. I can't believe you've been taking counsel from Mohamud, a criminally and mentally ill drug addict, spouting fake patriotism, toxic hatred, avalanches of lies, rambling nonsense, an insatiable, malignant narcissist, cult leader, overlord, fascist, nativist turd, traitor and coward. And worse, you would have me marry his repugnant daughter!"

"Fazza, you go too far."

"Too far? It was Zayed who went too far. He should have fought to be free to love. Our brother abdicated instead of standing up to our father. Zayed could have united to rule with Charlie as his wife. He could have made her his equal. He could have changed the constitution and made her his queen. Avana was their kingdom to rule. They should have stood together, just as we must stand together and let love, not fear, rule."

"Zayed should have had more tenacity and conviction. Our people would have respected his courage and their conviction. They would have admired his and Charlie's love just as they admire the love you and Melanie share and accept your right to rule. So don't give me all this crap about needing to marry someone I don't love to keep the peace."

CHAPTER FOURTEEN

"About yesterday—" Fazza said, entering Grace's bedroom.

"Don't you think we should get down to business?" Grace said, resisting the urge to ask, 'Don't you ever knock?' What was the point? It was his palace, his rules.

"The children. Yes, of course. Why didn't you say you are ready to be impregnated."

Grace exhaled loudly and rolled her eyes. "Honestly, what part of me telling you I don't want your children can't you hear? Being a mother conflicts with my career. And while I admire your persistence greatly," Grace said, lavishing her tone with sweeps of sarcasm, "Time is against us. Three days, you said. Three days to negotiate the future of Ferrari. But instead, you play games. You distract, stall, and focus on the impossible."

"I seem to recall you providing the distraction and very welcome it was too." He ran his thumb down her chin.

She made a soft, juddering sound. "It was a mistake."

"A mistake," he murmured. "How delicious." His eyes never left her face as his thumb grazed the flesh of her throat, tormenting her with the lightness of his touch, the promise in that small, gentle contact.

She closed her eyes. "The negotiations?" The question emerged as a tortured whisper. "How should we proceed?"

"Go to bed, *azeezi*," he whispered.

She shook her head slowly, her eyes opening to find him staring at her, his gaze loaded with purpose.

Her eyes roamed his face. "Were you even serious about the acquisition of Ferrari?"

He nodded slowly. "Very serious." He stepped forward, causing her to retreat toward the bed.

"Why?" she challenged.

"Why? Because I desire you."

"Why Ferrari?" she asked stubbornly.

"I have my reasons."

"'Which are?"

He shrugged.

"You're a property developer and a philanthropist focused on democracy, education, and anti-discrimination. What do you need with Ferrari?"

His fingers ached to plunge into her thick, silken hair, press her back against the soft, feather-filled mattress, and make love to her. Instead, he forced his pulse to still, summoning all his willpower and balling his fists at his side. Perhaps if they got the negotiations out of the way, they could make love later.

"Very well, let us talk business."

"Not here," she said, staring at the bed. "Don't you have somewhere more suitable?"

His eyes glittered. "Somewhere we can focus? Somewhere we won't be disturbed?"

"Yes," she said. "That's exactly what I had in mind."

"Very well, as you wish. We leave tonight."

"Leave?"

"By camel."

"*By camel*?" she recoiled. "Those stubborn, stinking, aggressive, unpredictable spitting missiles ejecting saliva filled with the contents of their three stomachs?"

"I'm joking. Get dressed and come to my office."

Fazza and Grace stood face to face in his study, their eyes locked in a battle of wills. It was clear from the onset that their personalities and cultural differences clashed.

With his regal demeanor and traditional Arabian attire, Fazza exuded an air of confidence and authority. He was in his element, on his turf, a ruler very much in command. On the other hand, Grace radiated a no-nonsense attitude, dressed in the sharp black business suit she had been wearing the day she'd been abducted.

Black, she decided, mirrored her determined and driven personality. She wasn't dressing for the desert or for the dreams she fleetingly indulged. She was dressing for success. She was negotiating to win.

As they sat in his office, Grace expressed her vision for Ferrari, emphasizing the need to cater to the evolving demands of the global market. She shared her insights into the automotive industry, highlighting the importance of maintaining Ferrari's brand identity while embracing innovation.

"So, Fazza, you believe Ferrari should focus more on luxury and exclusivity," Grace said, her voice tinged with skepticism. "But what about innovation and embracing sustainable technologies? The automobile industry constantly evolves, and we must adapt to stay ahead. Ferrari's customers and fans are driven by their passion for technological innovation while pursuing excellence in design and craftsmanship. They want change, not cleaving to the past."

Fazza crossed his arms, his expression unyielding. "Ferrari's heritage is built on craftsmanship and elegance. We must preserve that reputation if we are to turn a profit, catering to the discerning few who appreciate the artistry and exclusivity of the brand. The market for electric vehicles and sustainable technologies is important but should not be our primary focus."

Grace's eyes narrowed, her determination shining through. "I understand the importance of heritage, but the world is changing. We need to embrace technological advancements to remain relevant and competitive. Our customers demand more environmentally friendly options, and we must deliver."

The tension in the room continued to escalate as their opposing visions collided. The clash of cultures and ideologies only exacerbated the already heated debate. Both Fazza and Grace were fiercely protective of their own vision and refused to back down.

Fazza's voice grew firmer as he defended his perspective. "I respect your passion for innovation, but Ferrari's core values lie in its exclusivity and performance. We cannot sacrifice those principles to cater to passing trends. We must remain true to our heritage."

"We," she fired. "You sound as though you have already purchased the company."

Grace's frustration mounted as she struggled to make him see her point of view. "Your Highness," she said, opting to defer to his title. Their personal history, while brief and regretfully intimate, was clouding their minds and their judgment.

"I more than anyone appreciate Ferrari's heritage, but we

cannot afford to be stagnant. We must adapt and evolve, or we risk being left behind. Our competitors are already investing heavily in electric vehicles and sustainable technologies."

Fazza's eyes flashed with a mix of determination and frustration. "I may be new to Ferrari, but I do know about performance cars, and I know what collectors with my vast wealth demand—and what they will not tolerate. We can explore sustainable technologies without compromising the essence of Ferrari. But we must prioritize the driving experience, the thrill, and the emotion our cars evoke. That is what sets a high-performance car apart."

Grace took a deep breath, her mind racing with potential solutions. "Your Highness, what if we find a way to strike a balance? We can continue producing the high-performance, luxurious cars Ferrari is known for while investing in research and development for electric and hybrid models. This way, we can cater to a wider range of customers without compromising our core values."

Fazza's expression softened slightly as he considered Grace's proposal. "The idea is not without merit," he conceded.

Their initial clash of personalities gradually transformed into a spirited debate. They challenged each other's ideas, each defending their own vision fervently. However, beneath the surface, mutual respect began to form. They admired each other's passion and determination, recognizing the potential of their collaboration.

Minutes turned into hours, and as the afternoon glided toward the end of the day, Grace and Fazza continued discussing strategy, analyzing market trends, and brainstorming ideas. They discovered a shared love for innovation, and their conversations became more animated and engaging.

The initial skepticism and professional boundaries melted, replaced by genuine connection.

Amidst the discussions, Fazza and Grace were drawn to each other's intellect, wit, and ambition. As they peeled back the layers of their professional facades, they realized that their connection ran more profound than just business and their obvious physical attraction.

Grace was acutely aware of the complexities ahead. Their different cultural backgrounds and the expectations placed upon them added another layer of complexity to their professional relationship. She knew that continuing to pursue a romantic connection could jeopardize their success and create a media frenzy, distracting from everything she had achieved in her career.

Yet, as they continued to work toward the rejuvenation of Ferrari's fortunes, their shared passion and growing admiration for each other became impossible to ignore. The line between personal admiration and professional respect blurred, and they stood at the precipice of a decision that could change their lives forever.

What if merging business and pleasure was exactly what they should do? Grace wondered for the first time if finding common ground in all aspects of their relationship could transform not just Ferrari's fortunes but their lives.

Just as she was warming to the idea of sharing her life with him, Fazza asked the unthinkable.

"When were you going to tell me you were married?"

CHAPTER FIFTEEN

race froze. Her fierce poise and radical acceptance that they could navigate their cultural differences wilted under the weight of his accusation.

"People always love to say, 'How can you expect someone else to love you (romantically) if you do not love yourself?' or 'If you learn to love yourself, everything else will fall into place.' I disagree with the first idea because sometimes I think a person needs to be shown that they are worthy enough for love before becoming capable of it."

"That's not what I asked you."

"Why are you angry with me? I'm not angry with you," she said.

"I'm not a divorcee, Grace. I'm not hiding a marriage."

"I wasn't hiding. My personal life is my own business, and I don't much care for the term divorcee."

"Married plus not married equals divorced."

"Young plus stupid equals mistake. If you add low self-esteem, the equation runs into a negative number. Majorally negative. I was 19. It was a lifetime ago. I don't want to live in the past."

"Who was he?"

"I told you. I don't want to talk about it."

"Him. He's a him. Not an it."

Grace sighed. "Are you going to make me relive a past I'd rather forget?"

"I need to know who you were and who you are, Grace."

"What does that have to do with our negotiations?"

"I only do business with people I trust."

She wrapped her arms around her chest and squeezed tight as though giving herself a hug for strength. "I struggled a lot when I was young. Then along came *him*. Looking back now, I was easy prey. A young woman starved of love. He was older. A lot older. He knew exactly what to say to manipulate me. As soon as we were married, he began controlling every aspect of my life. My friends. My career. My finances. I'd really rather not go into it. Trust me when I say it was ugly love. I was lucky to escape with my life."

"I'm sorry. I didn't mean to retraumatize you."

"You didn't know, and I liked it that way. And now you'll probably think less of me. I mean, what sort of person gets caught up with a loser—and marries him."

"You're being hard on yourself."

"Others were. Others will be. That's why I don't talk about it. Not because I'm trying to be deceptive but because I want to put my energy into who I am and who I want to be. I'm not that broken, frightened young woman anymore. And while it might be true that others will think I am fatally flawed, I know that my relationship with myself is the longest love affair I'll ever have. I know this is love I can trust. I also know it's hard work. *I'm hard work.*"

"No. You're anything but hard work, trust me."

Trust. There was that six-letter word again, thrown around so casually. No, she couldn't trust. Not like she had. Not so easily. Trust had to be earned. How exactly? She was still figuring that out. But they were off to a good start. Dare she admit it? *Fazza felt safe. And that felt as uncomfortable as it felt good.*

"For many people, like me, self-love does not come easily," she said. "It involves forward, backward, and sideways steps. It's a non-linear process we'll be working on our whole lives. Parts of it will be ugly and involve doing hard things, like putting ourselves in situations that trigger anxiety, trauma, discomfort, and maybe even self-loathing. But that's OK. Because if, like me, you sometimes find all the self-love discourse transforms into just another stick to beat yourself with, we can try something else. Something less loaded and less radical for those of us with brains that struggle."

"Is that how you feel when you're with me? That you're doing an ugly dance, putting yourself in harm's way? That I'm a stick to beat yourself with so that you can heal? I'm not sure I like playing the villain."

"You're not the villain, Fazza. Just the opposite. If I felt that way, I wouldn't have stayed and indulged your charade of abducting me."

"Really?" he lobbied, disbelievingly. "Not even if it meant you could catch a prince?"

Her gaze met his, and her heart lurched at the vulnerability she saw in Fazza's eyes. She suddenly realized he'd spent his whole life thinking people wanted something from him. How must it feel to have stratospheric wealth, astounding looks, and royal status? To have it all and genuinely believe nobody wants you for who you are but for what they can get?

"I wasn't trying to catch a prince, Fazza. I was trying to catch myself. To love myself. To find out if I was lovable. I decided long ago that it's just about renaming the concept.

So, instead of self-love, the thing I'm looking forward to trying out is self-warmth. Warmth is easier to imagine. It's a much more ordinary visual. The idea of coming to a fire after the bitter cold of a winter's day, the warmth of a hot meal when you're exhausted, or that sense of comfort you feel on summer days when you're with the people who make you feel safe. I've decided self-warmth can't punish or set off 'should' spirals in your brain. It's also much easier to come back to. If blasts of icy cold and frozen ground arrive, just grab a blanket. Make yourself cozy. And only later think about the mountains you have to climb."

She glanced at the framed portrait on the wall behind his desk of his brothers sitting around a fire enjoying a traditional meal in the desert.

"Self-warmth is little moments. Good food. Laughter," she said. "Letting yourself sleep when you're tired. Following your impulses and your whims. But you have to start gently. *I have to start gently.* Slowly," she added. "Fires take time to light. The sun sometimes takes a while before its rays can be felt, but eventually, they will land on your skin. You will feel them on your face. And when you do, you will relish it. You will hold it tightly to yourself like a glowing fragment of light to be put inside your chest, which you can pull out to look at if the weather changes."

"We can do this, Grace. One step at a time," Fazza said, wrapping his arms around her. "I'm looking forward to my life getting warmer with you. I can't think of anyone I'd rather journey with on this crazy ride called love. Are you in? Will you join me?"

And this time, Grace didn't fight. She folded in his embrace, and for the first time in her life, she felt safe.

CHAPTER SIXTEEN

Fazza hadn't been joking when he mentioned journeying into the desert on camelback. Rather than repulse her, it was the most erotic, sensuous thing she'd ever experienced.

In the vast Arabian desert, under the sparkling night sky, her arms and legs wrapped around him, rocking and swaying in harmony with the giant beast, she mentally prepared for the intimacy she knew with certainty lay ahead. The desert winds whispered softly, carrying the scent of sensuality.

They dismounted near a crackling fire, which cast a warm glow around them both. The prince's eyes were filled with desire as he gazed into Grace's, reflecting the flickering flames.

"Fires take time to flame," he murmured.

"Slowly," she added.

With a gentle touch, he traced his fingers along the curves of her face, cherishing the beauty before him. As the fire danced, casting shadows upon the sand, their lips met in a passionate kiss, igniting a flame within their hearts.

Embraced by the desert's enchanting tranquility, they

slowly began to undress, their bodies revealing vulnerability and desire.

Trust, Grace whispered inwardly as she allowed herself to be seen and embraced in her most authentic and unguarded state. As each article of clothing was removed, she shed more layers of inhibition, ready to fully reveal her true self to Fazza.

Her skin shimmered like moonlit sand. Fazza's touch was both tender and commanding. The cool desert breeze caressed their bare bodies, heightening their senses and deepening their connection.

Lying down on a soft blanket beneath the stars, Fazza and Grace became one with the desert's timeless beauty.

She cried out, welcoming his length, as their bodies moved in perfect harmony, their love unfolding with every rhythmic thrust. The sand beneath them molded to their desires, cradling their bodies like a sacred sanctuary.

As the night wore on, their love-making intensified, reaching heights she had never experienced. The stars above seemed to shine brighter, the fire crackled and danced, mirroring the flames of their passion.

In this oasis of love and intimacy, Grace surrendered herself to him, trusting in the power of their connection. Under the stars, their love soared, transcending the boundaries of time and space.

Fazza and Grace lay entwined, their bodies basking in the afterglow of their union. The Arabian desert had witnessed their love, and the memories of that night would forever be etched in their hearts. But that, she reminded herself, could only ever be temporary—a wonderful memory celebrating their successful negotiations.

"This changes nothing," she said, needing to hear those words herself as she needed him to accept her resolute decision.

He pushed up from the sand and looked at her, his eyes hooded and impossible to read. His cheeks were dark, slashed with the blood-orange glow of the dying fire. "I am aware of that, *habibti.*"

She turned from him, noticing with shock the plume of dust trailing from the rapidly approaching Range Rover.

His head jerked in the direction of the car. "My driver will take us back."

CHAPTER SEVENTEEN

ere those his children? Grace wondered as she watched Fazza the following day, kicking a ball along the beach, followed by two laughing boys. From their height, she guessed they were aged six or seven, and they were identical twins. He hadn't mentioned children, but then why would he? They barely knew anything about each other.

If the boys were his, he had kept them a secret away from the prying eyes of a ravenous media. George and Amal Clooney's twins were seldom seen in newspapers. Protecting their privacy was important to them, and sometimes it was as though they didn't exist.

How would she feel about Fazza if he did have children with another woman? Another wife? Wouldn't he have said? Sheikhs had multiple wives, multiple children, multiple lives, Grace reminded herself. It was as if it was deeply entrenched in their culture that one wife was never enough. But look out if a woman wanted another husband or strayed from the marital harem. What hypocrisy!

What number wife would she be, she wondered if she was

forced to marry Fazza. Wife 63? She grimaced. It wasn't a life she wanted. *Ever.* Besides, now that he had possessed her, it seemed his interest had waned. Had she been too quick to trust him? Her body throbbed with remembered pleasure.

She watched him allow the smaller boy to tackle Fazza, wrapping his tiny hands around Fazza's ankles and forcing him to fall into the soft sand. If the children with him now were his, he was a good father, she decided.

The boy's twin brother sat on his belly. No, she corrected, you wouldn't call that firm stomach below those firm six-pack abs a belly. Bellies were soft and spongy and round. Grace rubbed her hand across her flat stomach. If she fell pregnant, she'd have a belly. Then how would Fazza feel about her? Some men went off their wives when their bodies changed after childbirth. She recalled a recent headline she'd seen, 'I'm not attracted to my wife when her body changed after she had my children.'

Would that alchemical fire they shared last night, that compelling, magnetic attraction, that undeniable sexual chemistry die when their child arrived?

When! What was she thinking?

If! she affirmed. *As if!*

She pressed against the plaster walls of the Little Palace. She didn't want Fazza to see her watching him with the children. What if he saw her longing? What if he saw the little smile that wouldn't stop every time Fazza and the children's whooping laughter reached her ears?

The sexy, purring sound Ferrari engines made was engineered to send arousal levels soaring, but now Fazza and the children's mirth reached deep into her belly and tickled her insides with longing. She realized with a jolt that the authentic sound of pure joy that some cars created artificially was as addictive as it was dangerous.

She leaned forward, powerless to turn away, watching with increasing happiness as Fazza kicked the ball high, then raced along the beach as the rainbow-striped ball began to fall. The pops of brilliant color and children's laughter, fizzing with uncensored bliss and the exuberant delight on Fazza's face, brought more joy to her life than she thought possible.

"Run! Catch it!" she called, realizing too late that cheer-leading the twins had revealed her hiding place.

Fazza glanced toward her. For a moment, time ceased to exist, his gaze entwined with hers in shared longing. Her body flamed with hot, urgent need as though he had reached inside her and discovered the most vulnerable part of her. The part that, against all reason, so badly wanted to be a mother and have his child.

She turned and retreated into the bedroom, but the hurtful, hopeful truth followed her.

What she would have given to be the apple of her daddy's eye.

What she would give to bear Fazza's child.

CHAPTER EIGHTEEN

"You seldom talk about your family," Fazza said the following day. He didn't want to talk about their lovemaking, admit his urgent need, or confess his fear she might disappear. She had told him their lovemaking hadn't changed anything, yet it had.

"Where do I begin?" she said. "With my disappointed parents when their much-longed-for son was a girl? 11 months later, when the golden child, my brother, was born, and I became the family scapegoat? With the bull shit aristocratic ancestry and all the spin about being born with a silver spoon in my mouth—only discovering when my grandparents left me out of their will that a girl could never inherit property despite being the oldest? Why would I speak about my family? They betrayed me."

Fazza remained silent. What consolation could he possibly offer? What words of comfort could he give? What salve could he rub on her lifetime of hurt that would heal her broken heart?

"I'm sorry," he said after reflective silence.

Grace's eyes flared. "Don't be. I'm nobody's victim. I refuse to be. Everything I've achieved, every accolade I've earned, is down to me. Fighting has made me stronger. I'm proud of that."

She was angry. He understood that. He'd said the wrong thing. She didn't want his pity. He'd fucked up. Now what?

"I'm sorry," he repeated.

She scowled.

"I'm sorry for saying 'I'm sorry.'" He stumbled over his words, hoping she would see beyond them and register his true intent—his compassion, care, and respect. Her fierce strength was to be admired, but her mistreatment was undeserved. She had been exposed to undeserved prejudice because of her gender. As the son of a king, he may have been born into privilege, but he hoped she would sense his shared understanding because childhood trauma was something he could identify with.

She sat stiffly, her hands fisted, her jaw locked, refusing to speak. Now what? How did they move forward? How did they stop the hurt that united them in pain and sorrow, preventing them from claiming the happiness and love he knew they could share?

If only—

If only they'd had different parents.

If only they didn't allow their past to define them.

If only she weren't so self-reliant and stubborn.

"I used to pray that my father would love me one day," Fazza offered. He noticed surprised acknowledgment flicker across her face. She turned, curiosity pooling in her vast emerald eyes.

"He never did. I tried to be the son he wanted. I saw how my brothers suffered trying to be themselves. My father was cruel, brutal, and uncompassionate. My brothers were my mother's favorites. I tried to be my father's chosen one. As I grew older, I molded myself into the man his cold heart could love. A lover of women. An arrogant playboy, collecting lingerie models with the same aloof indifference my father had. Caring for nothing—not their hopeful hearts, distant dreams, or missives of marriage. I was fueled only by successful conquests. And the Lamborghinis I collected with the same insatiable greed as women? I never cared for them. They were my father's passion. I don't give a shit about cars."

She turned, realization flaring in her eyes. "The Ferraris?"

"All for you."

"The company?" She gulped as though shame and guilt caught in her throat. "I made you purchase something you never wanted."

"No! I want what I want. I make my own choices. If purchasing a Ferrari was what it took to have you, swapping allegiance from my despot father's loyalty to Lamborghini, what did I care? What did I care if I had to buy the whole dammed company? I would have brought the Soviet Union's Lada brand just to be close to you."

"Lada!" Grace's face twisted in horror.

"I'm being dramatic. But if that were what it took, I would've bought it. So, this family of yours? The one you never speak about."

She shrugged.

"I told you about mine. I shared my family history. Isn't it time you reciprocated?"

"It's not interesting."

"Humor me."

"It's not funny."

"Indulge me."

"There once was a girl who wasn't loved—" she began.

But you are.

"Go on," he gently urged.

"I don't want to be vulnerable. I don't want to put my heart out there."

"Let the walls down. Be a little less guarded. I won't judge."

And she told him everything. Her Cinderella life with all her dreams, her lonely childhood, the cruel, tormenting siblings, and her mother's unpredictable rages hurling hateful words like swords, splintering her soft, sensitive soul into shards of glass.

"Your inner child needs nurturing," he offered.

A frown crested her brow as she looked at him. "You sound like my counselor."

"It's always interesting to me," Fazza continued, "How people's names sometimes define them. Grace Hunt is the huntress archetype. She is fiercely independent, self-motivated, competent, and emotionally unassailable. She is the woman who places excessive importance on her personal performance."

"I thought you said you weren't going to judge."

"I see you because I see me. That was how I have been: driven by my false ego, unable to give birth to new parts of myself, wishing but not knowing how to embody a new sense of peace."

She looked into his eyes, her fierce veneer brieflyā slipping, revealing the kindness, compassion, and tenderness he knew she possessed. Her eyelids fluttered. He recognized the huntress fiercely clinging to her old identity. He recognized all of that because he saw it in himself.

"It's Easter, isn't it?" he said, glancing at the date on his watch: Thursday, March 29th, the day before Good Friday. "What is that thing you Westerners love to do? That game with the chocolate eggs?"

"An Easter Egg Hunt," she said.

"My brother's sons would love that."

CHAPTER NINETEEN

is brother's sons.

The three words brought unexpected relief. The two young boys who brought so much happiness were Fazza's nephews, not his children, she reflected as she stood on the beach that following evening. Life and soul- that is what Fazza and the children brought to her—life and soul and love. The realization shocked and surprised her.

Grace dug her bare feet into the sand, feeling the warmth between her toes and the gentle breeze rustling through her hair. Ever since Fazza had come into her life, the world looked softer and more beautiful, she mused as the setting sun cast a golden shimmer over the waters of the Arabian Gulf. She took a deep breath, inhaling the balmy salty air, and smiled. It was a perfect evening for an adventure with the young Arab princes who had captured her heart.

Fazza was right; she needed to embrace her inner child, and he had been so helpful and considerate. He had ensured Grace had everything she needed to surprise her nephews. The chefs had prepared marshmallow easter eggs covered in dark chocolate and wrapped them in unique insulating material so they wouldn't melt in the desert heat. His brother's wife, Lucy, had stopped by earlier in the day with some artist's materials and helped her create a special toy from her childhood.

She reached into her oversized bag and rubbed the silk ribbons of the paper kites in her fingers. It was funny how her memory played tricks on her, forcing from her heart the few happy, magical moments her father and she had shared flying kites in Central Park on windy days. Now, rays of light illuminating her dark past were coming back. And it was all thanks to Fazza and his family and this magical place.

As Grace approached the boys, skimming pearls at the water's edge, she could see their excitement as they turned and saw her. Ahmed and Omar, dressed in long white *dishdashis*, ran towards her, their laughter filling the air. Grace knelt to their level, her heart filled with joy.

"Are you ready for some fun, my little princes?" she asked, her voice filled with anticipation.

The boys nodded enthusiastically, their eyes shining. Grace reached into her bag and pulled out two colorful kites. She handed one to Ahmed, who took it with a wide grin. Omar took the other and tugged at Grace's hand, pulling her along the long stretch of beach.

Grace watched as the boys ran and giggled, their laughter rising with the kites soaring above them, the rainbow ribbons gaily trailing through the air. She couldn't help but giggle, feeling a sense of freedom and joy in their presence. It was as if those rare moments of innocence and playfulness of her childhood had been awakened.

As the sun dipped lower in the darkening sky, she led the boys to a secluded spot on the beach fringed by palms, where they sat down in the sand. Grace reached into her bag again and pulled out a small box filled with tiny water jars, colorful paints, and brushes.

"Let's create something beautiful," she said as she handed the boys some hard-boiled eggs still in their shells. "Something your mom and dad and the rest of your family can enjoy when we share a meal later."

"What fun!" The boys chorused, their eyes widening with excitement as they dipped their brushes into the vibrant hues. Grace grinned as they painted their masterpieces, their tiny hands covered in paint. They laughed and cheered as their creations became more elaborate with each stroke.

Grace felt a deep sense of healing within herself as the boys continued to paint. She realized that playing with the young princes was bringing joy not only to their lives but also to her own. It was a reminder that she deserved to embrace her inner child and find happiness in the simplest of moments.

She closed her eyes, took deep breaths, and fully immersed herself in the moment's transformation and tranquility. As she focused on her breath, Grace became aware of a faint whisper in the depths of her being. It was the voice of her inner child, a part of her that had long been neglected and wounded. The voice was timid, filled with pain and longing for healing.

Grace opened her heart to her inner child with a gentle smile, inviting her to come forward and be heard. Slowly, a small, fragile figure emerged from the shadows. The child's eyes were filled with tears, and her body trembled with vulnerability. "I'm here for you," Grace whispered. "I want to help you heal."

The child hesitated for a moment, unsure of whether to trust Grace. But the warmth and sincerity in her eyes were undeniable. With a glimmer of hope, the child took Grace's hand, feeling a sense of safety and solace in her touch.

Grace understood that healing the inner child required more than listening and empathizing. It needed nurturing, love, and acceptance. Wasn't that precisely what Fazza had given her, she mused as she slowly opened her eyes. He saw through her mask and her barrier; he saw the strong woman she was and the little girl she had been, the wounded girl full of fear and hope and longing. He saw all of her—deserving of love, happiness, and all the good things life has to offer.

"Let's build a sandcastle," she said to the boys, wanting to reconnect again with the inner joy and playfulness they embraced so effortlessly. Grace stood up and extended her hand to them. Together, they ran towards the water, their laughter filling the air.

Grace listened intently to the stories the boys shared as they rested on the beach, erecting their castle with mounds of sand. They spoke of their adventures in their imaginary kingdom, their bravery in the face of danger, and the importance of family, love, and friendship. The innocence in their voices reminded Grace of the childlike wonder and imagination that Grace had lost over the years.

As the evening wore on, Grace decided it was the perfect time to surprise the boys with the Easter egg hunt. "Turn around, cover your eyes, and wait until I call you," she said, standing up. "Promise me you won't peek."

"We promise," they said, spinning to face the sea.

She ran along the sand, scattering the colorfully wrapped marshmallow eggs across the beach, hiding them in the dunes and behind palm trees.

"You can look now," she called. "It's a hunt. Let's see how many Easter Eggs you can find."

The boys squealed with delight as they discovered each hidden treasure, their laughter echoing through the night.

With the last egg found and the moon rising high above them, Grace gathered the boys in her arms. They sat together on the beach, their hearts filled with love and joy.

At that moment, Grace realized that she had not only created a magical experience for the young princes but had also healed more of herself.

As they watched the waves gently kiss the shore, Grace wished that if she were to have a child with Fazza, they too would have memories like this: simple pleasures, unhurried moments filled with a newfound sense of joy and a playful spirit.

She whispered a silent thank you to the Arabian beach, the young princes, Fazza, and the healing power of play. The memories they had created together would forever be cherished, a reminder that amid life's challenges, there was always room for laughter, love, and the rediscovery of one's inner child.

"Let's build a sandcastle," she said to the boys, wanting to reconnect again with the inner joy and playfulness they embraced so effortlessly. Grace stood up and extended her hand to them. Together, they ran towards the water, their laughter filling the air.

CHAPTER TWENTY

"What is Easter?" Ahmed asked as she rose to her feet.

Grace hesitated and sat back down. She pressed her lips into a firm line, uncertain what to say to the curious seven-year-old prince. "Easter is—"

"Easter is a significant holiday for Christians," Fazza replied, his voice resonating with sincerity as he sat on the sand beside her.

She turned to him, relief etched on her face. What a beautiful enigma she was, he thought briefly—fun and formidable, playful and serious, soulful and steely. He sensed she didn't want to talk about things that had the potential to be misunderstood. Religious and spiritual views brought comfort to so many but also had such a corrosive power to divide.

He felt it was better he approached the subject. Besides, Grace was supposed to be discovering her inner child, not giving a religious sermon. He glanced at her, thinking as he did so how beautiful she looked, bathed in golden light.

"Christians believe in a man called Christ, also known as Jesus. Easter holds deep spiritual meaning for Christians. It is a time of reflection, repentance, and gratitude for the man they call their savior, who made the ultimate sacrifice when he—" Fazza hesitated.

The true enemies were not people but ideology, hatred, and ignorance, but how much knowledge should he share? Grace and the boys had been having so much fun flying kites, painting Easter eggs, and laughing. How could he reconcile that Easter marked the time the Christians believed Jesus was betrayed by his disciple, arrested, tried, and executed—nailed to a cross while his killers watched, and now they were playing games, eating chocolate, and celebrating Easter? How could he explain any of this? Or that Christians believed that Jesus didn't die but was resurrected?

Grace looked at Fazza, imploring him with her glittering emerald eyes to spare the princes the ghastly tale of Jesus's crucifixion.

"One day, Jesus died," he said. "But because he was so special, he was born again in a place they call heaven."

"Is that where my kite is flying to?" Omar asked, pointing to the tail of rainbow ribbons fluttering above the horizon toward a bright, dazzling star sparkling like diamonds.

"Yes," Fazza said. "That's exactly it. The kite is like the gift Jesus left his believers—he watches over them and promises eternal peace when they die."

"And forgiveness if they are sorry for any naughty things they have done, " Grace added. Islam also strongly emphasizes repentance, forgiveness, and the importance of doing good deeds. During Ramadan, Muslims fast, pray, and engage in acts of charity to strengthen their faith and seek forgiveness." She paused, allowing her words addressing the similarities between Easter and Muslim Arab traditions to sink in.

Fazza could see the princes listening intently, their expressions reflecting a mix of curiosity and respect.

"While Easter is centered around the resurrection of Jesus, Islam doesn't share the belief in his divinity. But both traditions emphasize the importance of faith, compassion, and love for humanity. Easter is also a time of joy, hope, and new beginnings. It is a reminder that even in the face of darkness, there is always light," Grace said.

"I didn't know you knew so much about Arabic culture," Fazza said, admiration deepening.

She leaned toward him, whispering in his ear so the children wouldn't hear. "Why would you? We barely know each other. I'm not an ignorant, close-minded bigot," she whispered. "I don't care if people believe in tall, blue men if it sustains them and brings peace." The sting of her words mingled with the fresh scent of the orange blossom notes in her perfume.

It was a fair call, he reprimanded himself, respecting her readiness to speak her mind and firmly but sweetly putting him in his place—and what a brilliant mind she had, too. A brilliant mind to match her equally brilliant body.

"It's important to respect different beliefs, nephews. By understanding and respecting each other's traditions, we can foster harmony and build bridges of mutual understanding. Through dialogue and empathy, we can appreciate the diversity of beliefs and cultures that enrich our world."

As Fazza finished his explanation, he could see the Arab princes nodding, their expressions reflecting a deeper understanding and appreciation for the significance of Easter for Christians and the shared values between the two faiths.

Fazza rose to his feet. "Now let's go and share another tradition Christians and Arabs love—sharing a meal!" He bent down and let Omar climb on his back.

"We can show Mommy and Daddy what we made for Easter, Uncle Fazza," Ahmed said, jumping up and taking his hand. He turned to Grace, reached for her fingers, and clasped them in his.

"Thank you for sharing your traditions with us," Ahmed and Omar said as they walked toward the palace. Fazza smiled, feeling a sense of unity and harmony between them. He was grateful to Grace for the opportunity to help bridge cultural gaps and foster understanding among different faiths.

He loved her more than his determination to keep her against her will. He loved her like she was tonight: full of fun, joy, passion, spark, and spirit.

He wanted to give her the most priceless thing possible. But what would she do with it?

CHAPTER TWENTY-ONE

"I heard you loved orchids, so I've bought you flowers," Fazza said the following morning. "My brother, Anwar, has quite a passion for them and grows a coveted collection of rare, exotic orchids. Many were on the verge of extinction. Perhaps one day, you may like to go and see them, but for now, I asked him to select the most exquisite, divine, and enigmatic orchid possible. A variety that captured your essence when I think about you and what you have come to mean to me."

"A black orchid!" Grace's gaze alighted on the magnificent blooms planted in a large crystal bowl as Fazza placed them on the table away from direct sunlight.

"Black represents the shadow, the depths, the mysterious. It is the immersion of all colors. It is the beauty, stillness, strength, and energy of a new moon in a black sky. It is the color of freedom."

She bent her head toward them and inhaled.

"They smell and look exquisite. How did you know I would love them?"

"It's my role to know what you desire."

She smiled. "Is it? I hadn't realized," she said, aware her tone was no longer frosty with annoyance at being the desert prince's captive. She was beginning to enjoy her life. She no longer saw a future of restriction and control but one full of adventures, ripe with possibility—and love.

"I didn't know orchids could be black. The center looks like a marshmallow Easter egg, with baby pink, daffodil yellows, and creamy white. They are absolutely delicious. Thank you."

His hands curved around her, making her feel delicate in his hold.

"Forgive me," he said, pulling away.

"There's nothing to forgive," she whispered. "You've given me the perfect gift. So many people think they can buy their way to love, bestowing priceless gems and exorbitantly priced treasures. But gifts from the heart don't need to be expensive. You've shown me so much love, the little things like these sweet orchids and the bigger things like the gift of play." She pressed her hands on his chest, so firm and warm.

"I've kept you here," he gritted. "Against your will."

She lifted her face toward him and sprinkled tiny kisses on his neck. "Against my will, you say," she murmured. A smile tilted the corners of her mouth, creating those desirable dimples on her cheeks.

He arched his back, wishing he did not have to say what he must say. Wishing he did not have to do what he must do. Wishing he had any other choice but the one thing fate demanded.

"It breaks my heart—" he began, "You're not making this easy. You look so delectable in the morning light."

She trailed her tongue over his lips.

"So ravishing."

Her nipples budded against her silk nightgown.

"Repentance," he said too quickly.

She took a shocked step backward, her hands trembling slightly, her eyes filled with fear and fierce resilience.

"I have been consumed with the obsessive quest to possess you."

"There is goodness within you. I know you regret what you've done."

"You have shown me a glimmer of light in the darkness. You have given me the strength to do what I must do."

He paced across the room, his eyes locked onto Grace's, revealing a flicker of remorse. " I wish it didn't have to be this way. If I could turn back time, I would have done it differently. Grace, you have seen the depths of my darkness, the lengths I would go to possess what I desire. But you are right. I am burdened by regret, haunted by my choices," he turned away from her and then spun around.

"I am my father's son," he gritted. "No different from the man I loath. My father who imprisoned his daughters."

"We are all capable of redemption, Fazza," Grace said, her voice filled with confusion and compassion. "It's never too late to right the wrongs we've committed. You've proved your love, over and over, in the short time we've had."

Fazza's brow furrowed, then transformed into a mixture of determination and sorrow. He reached into his pocket, retrieving a set of keys. "No! I have held you captive, denying you the freedom you deserve. It was a selfish act capturing you, driven by selfish desire. But tonight, I will amend my wrongs."

He approached Grace, the keys jingling in his trembling hand. "Your Ferrari, it's in the courtyard. "Fly free, my darling. I release you from this gilded cage."

CHAPTER TWENTY-TWO

Three months later…

L ove is blooming. Grace stared into the new orchid flower on her desk, narrowing her focus to the insides, which were yellow and pink, reminding her of that magical Easter egg hunt she had shared with Fazza's nephews only three months before.

How ironic. Fazza bought me these flowers, handed me the keys to his Ferrari, and all but commanded me to drive out of his life, and now another flower is blooming. What is it trying to tell me?

Maybe we are meant to be together.

She pushed the thought from her mind and turned her attention back to the spreadsheets and sales graphs. Ferrari's fortunes had taken an upward turn thanks to her business alliance with Fazza. He had honored his decision to invest in Ferrari, but what did any of it mean? What did career success, accolades, and fortune matter without Fazza's love?

She needed to reignite the spark. She needed a break from

always thinking about dominating the business world and obsessing about cars, cars, cars!

She loved Ferrari—loved—past tense. The realization snuck up on her quietly. There was no gut punch, no searing certainty, just the peaceful, calm realization that she didn't need to prove anything to anyone anymore. Just like the orchids didn't need to prove anything, either.

She had reached the top. Now what?

Everything has its day. Even flowers fade. It was time for something new—something she always wanted to do—to become a mother, a wife, a lover, and a ruler with her husband and embark on passion projects that scattered joy, not pain, around the world.

But would he marry her? Did he even want her anymore?

She remembered how she had once said, 'I'll do anything for love—just don't make me give up Ferrari. The Passion. The status. The admiration. But she wasn't giving it up. She was simply letting go. Letting go of the need to prove to her parents she was worthy. Letting go of the need to gain everyone's approval. Letting go of the belief that to be loved, she had to over-achieve.

Just like Fazza had let her go, and while she had been hurt and angry, with the passage of time, she understood. He could not keep her if her love was not given freely. She had proved her point. She could not be bought by the Sheikh.

She glanced at her watch. Her passion for Ferrari had morphed into a new project now—becoming an angel investor and providing seed money for women entrepreneurs. Her new protégé was due any moment now. It was a timely and pleasant distraction as she figured out what to do.

She glanced again at the orchids.

You are meant to be together, they silently whispered.

CHAPTER TWENTY-THREE

"This is the opportunity of a lifetime," Poppy said inwardly as she stood before the grand entrance of the Ferrari headquarters, her heart pounding with excitement.

Ethan, the fashion tycoon she'd met in Montana, had sent samples of her lipstick to his wealthy friends—and now she had been commissioned by Grace Hunt, the CEO of Ferrari, to create a one-of-a-kind lipstick color called Ferrari Red.

She took a deep breath, adjusted her signature red beret, and entered the extravagant building. The foyer was adorned with sleek, modern designs that reflected the elegance and power of the Ferrari brand. As she approached the reception desk, Poppy marveled at the craftsmanship and attention to detail. Grace Hunt's personal assistant greeted her with a warm smile and escorted her to Grace's office.

Grace was everything Poppy hoped she would be—stylish and charismatic. As Poppy entered her office, Grace greeted her affectionately as though they were lifelong friends. The walls were covered with images of Ferraris in various shades of red, inspiring Poppy's creativity even further.

"Poppy, It's a pleasure to meet you finally," she said, extending her hand. "I've heard so much about your talent as a lipstick designer. Creating a lipstick color exclusively for Ferrari is a significant undertaking, and Ethan assures me you are the perfect person for the job."

Poppy's face flushed with pride as she shook Grace's hand. "It's a huge honor to be chosen for the launch of the new cosmetic line."

Grace nodded approvingly. "Ferrari is more than just a brand; it symbolizes power, passion, and elegance. We needed to diversify—all the great brands do, and I am assured you are the perfect person to take us there."

Poppy listened intently, her mind already racing with ideas. "I completely understand, Ms. Hunt."

"Grace. Please, call me Grace."

"Grace," she said, loving the beauty and strength of her name. "I believe we can achieve that by creating a vibrant yet sophisticated red. It should be a shade that commands attention, just like a Ferrari speeding down the racetrack."

Grace smiled, clearly intrigued. "I love your vision, Poppy. Now, let's delve into the details. I want the lipstick to have a matte finish, as it adds a touch of modernity. The formula should be long-lasting, ensuring the color stays vibrant throughout the day. And, of course, it should be enriched with nourishing ingredients to keep our lips feeling luxurious. And kissable—able to endure the most passionate kiss."

Poppy nodded, "Absolutely," she said, taking notes as Grace spoke. She wanted to capture every detail and ensure that the final product would be nothing short of perfection. "I will work closely with my team of chemists and color experts to create a unique formula that meets all of your requirements. We will experiment with different pigments and textures to achieve the desired result."

Grace leaned back in her chair, a glimmer of excitement in her eyes. "I have full confidence in your abilities, Poppy. I believe you will create a lipstick color that not only represents Ferrari but also becomes a coveted item in the beauty industry. The world has become so enamored with war. We need to experience the power and passion and joy of Ferrari Red lipstick just like women did during The Resistance."

Poppy felt a surge of determination as she looked into Grace's eyes. "I promise you, Ms. Hunt, I will pour my heart and soul into this project. Ferrari Red will be a shade that captivates the world and leaves a lasting impression."

Grace watched the young woman leave and rubbed her hand across her belly. Belly, not stomach, she affirmed, because love was blooming inside her. If only Fazza knew. What to do? It was all so confusing, not helped one bit by the maelstrom of fluctuating hormones assaulting her.

Heart and soul.

Poppy's words vibrated through her.

Had Grace, too, become enamored with war, fortifying herself with steely resistance, waging a war of silence, refusing to tell Fazza she loved him?

If she didn't tell Fazza how she felt, how everything had faded to grey, like a cloud masking the sun, without his love, what then? If she didn't tell him she was carrying his child, a child conceived under the stars, beside a warm fire, with love freely given by a woman in love—not by an untamed wife that had been bought—then everything would be lost.

A child would not know his father's love.

A father would not know his child's love.

A man would not know a woman's love.

His woman—blossoming with a fragrant, everlasting love *for him and their child.*

She shut her laptop and snatched her Birkin handbag, thrusting her hands inside and extracting the key to her Ferrari. She had to tell him the truth. She had everything now to lose. She had to risk it all—looking like a fool, possible rejection, the end of it all.

But rain and sunshine make the flowers grow, she affirmed, picking up the orchid firmly rooted in the crystal bowl Fazza had gifted.

Love is the core of divine creation, and if I hide away, focusing on my career, short-circuiting the only chance I'll ever have to love unconditionally, I'll never discover love's destiny for me.

CHAPTER TWENTY-FOUR

"There are no mistakes in love, only lessons," Fazza whispered to Grace as she lay in his arms that night.

She hadn't told him about their child yet. She wanted to curate the moment. To ensure everything was perfect. And she hadn't wanted to come running back to the palace shouting about her pregnancy. She needed to be sure that he loved her, to be certain she was the woman he wanted—not purely because she was carrying his child.

"You have surprised me, and now I wish to reciprocate. Pack a bag," he said simply, refusing to elaborate.

He was being so mysterious. So evasive. So secretive. What was this surprise Fazza had planned?

Three days later, Grace found herself in a picturesque palazzo nestled in the hills outside Venice. Little did she know that her life was about to change forever.

As the sun set, casting a warm glow over the lavish estate, Grace took a moment to admire the breathtaking view of

Venice in the distance. The gentle breeze carried the sweet scent of red roses, filling the air with an intoxicating fragrance. Unbeknownst to her, a rare gift awaited her arrival.

She dressed in the stunning crimson silk gown laid out for her on the bed. Red—the color of passion and love. Her eyes sparkled with excitement. Her heart fluttered with anticipation as she made her way down the elegant staircase, her footsteps echoing through the palazzo.

She gasped as she stepped outside. The sight that greeted her was nothing short of extraordinary. A vibrant red Ferrari with a sky-blue stripe running playfully down its bonnet stood before her, gleaming in the fading Venetian light, overflowing with red roses.

"Fazza!" she cried as the door to the Ferrari swung open.

Dressed impeccably in a tailored black suit, he exuded an air of confidence as he stepped from the car.

"*Marhabaan, habibti*. Hello, my love," he said, his voice carrying a hint of nervousness.

Grace's heart raced as Fazza took her hand and bent on one knee.

"Grace, will you accompany me on a journey filled with love, adventure, and shared dreams?" he asked, his eyes filled with sincerity. "Will you be my partner in life, my co-pilot, and my queen of forever love?"

Tears welled in her eyes.

How strange that three days ago, she had vowed she was ready to be a mother, a wife, and co-ruler, and in return, she would give up her role at Ferrari, not because he demanded it but because she wanted to. It was as if the winds of fate had heard her release her fears and dare to dream of love.

She looked into Fazza's eyes, seeing the depth of his emotions and the genuine love he held for her.

With a trembling voice, she replied, "Yes, my love, a

thousand and one yes's. I would love to join you as your wife on the greatest ride of all."

She glanced down at the huge Princess Diana sapphire ring encircled with diamonds as Fazza slid it on her index finger.

"Together, we will send love letters to the world, sharing our passion for each other and the creation of a better world."

With those words, Fazza pulled Grace close, enveloping her in an embrace filled with the promise of eternal love. They sealed their commitment with a kiss, their hearts entwined like the winding roads ahead, ready to conquer the world together, one red rose at a time.

CHAPTER TWENTY-FIVE

Where was he? Fazza should have been home hours ago.

Grace glanced at her watch. What was keeping him? Her stomach clenched. Something wasn't right. Mr. Punctual was never late.

It was Christmas. He promised her this year would be special. Special because it was their first Christmas as an engaged couple, special because she was pregnant. But Fazza didn't know that. How could he? Tonight was the night she was finally going to tell him. She picked up the gift box lovingly wrapped in baby blue. Inside were the results of the three-month scan she had secretly ordered confirming their child's sex.

Secrecy.

The word didn't sit well with her. As much as she adored Fazza's brothers' wives and understood their reasons for keeping their pregnancy a secret, she didn't want Fazza to discover she was carrying his child, a boy, his heir by accident.

Accident!

She felt her eyes flare wide. She scanned the infinite horizon. Where was Fazza?

Perhaps there was heavy traffic on the road leading from Aibud, she thought, trying to console herself. She told herself that the motorway leading from the desert metropolis was always jammed, not believing a word. Or maybe he had stopped to refuel?

She picked up her cellphone. "Siri, call Fazza," she commanded. Her teeth caught on her long nail as she placed a finger in her mouth. The unconscious gesture transported her to her childhood when she had crawled under the bed, out of harm's way, during one of her father's alcoholic tirades, coming out only when the police arrived and promised everything would be OK.

And then she saw them. The unmistakable red and blue neon lights winding across the desert towards the palace.

CHAPTER TWENTY-SIX

*T*hank God. He was alive.

Fazza lay motionless in the hospital, his eyes flickering in and out of consciousness.

"Oh my darling, I'm so sorry. It's all my fault."

Fear and guilt washed in her gut. If anything happened to him, Grace pushed her anxiety firmly aside. She sat beside him and gently wiped his forehead, willing him to survive. "You'll be ok," she whispered, projecting her voice with confidence, desperately willing him to live.

Then Melanie and Tariq were beside her, telling her the accident wasn't her fault, reassuring her that Fazza was strong and would live. Grace squeezed Fazza's hand and gently stroked his hair. She didn't know how long they'd been there when his fingers slowly flexed under hers.

"Grace." It was the tiniest whisper. He didn't open his eyes, but a line creased between his brows as if he were struggling to consciousness.

"I'm here, my darling. I'm here," she cried.

"Don't," he whispered breathlessly.

She bent closer to his lips to catch whatever he was trying to say.

"If I'm badly hurt. . .if I die."

"Don't! Don't say that. You are not going anywhere. Not without me. I need you, Fazza," she insisted passionately. The words she had wanted to say for so long now poured forth in a tidal wave of emotion.

"I'm carrying your child. Your son. Your heir."

He barely registered the words.

Why the hell hadn't she said them before?

His eyes flickered partially open. Pain glazed his eyes, excruciating pain. "My son?" His breath rasped as though his lungs pooled with blood.

"Yes," she whispered. "I'm pregnant with your child. We need you."

The nurse stood at Fazza's side and inserted a hypodermic syringe into his arm. Then another. Shooting him full with emergency morphine.

"We will not let you die," Grace said fiercely. She must summon the strength for both of them. For the three of them, she corrected, pressing her palm upon her belly.

"We conceived a child that night, beside the fire, beneath the stars, in the desert. You can't die, do you hear me? You can't die. I won't let you."

There seemed to be a slight flicker of recognition in his dulling eyes.

"Our son must know his father," she said with desperate vehemence. "You've got to live."

His lids dropped shut as if they were too heavy to hold open. Grace didn't know if he had heard. She had held back from telling him until she'd passed the twelve-week mark and was absolutely sure the baby was safe. Now, she regretted her decision. She should have told him earlier. He should have known. Perhaps he never would have left the Palace in that damned car. She never thought she would be praying both her unborn child and the man she loved would live.

"Our baby needs you," she called after him as strong arms wrapped around her and lifted her to her feet as the man who had come to mean more to her than life itself was transported to the operating theatre.

CHAPTER TWENTY-SEVEN

The weeks passed in a blur. For days on end, Fazza was x-rayed, poked, and prodded. Just when he thought it was over, it started again. Finally, the diagnosis came back. The internal bleeding has been stemmed, he was fit and healthy enough to leave. Love had healed him, he was sure of it. And to prove it, he vowed, he would marry Grace without a moment's delay. He had cheated death and seeded new life. He would be a husband and a father. It was more than he ever dreamed.

The sun rose like a balloon, casting a golden hue over the palace. Grace stood outside the walls as Fazza had asked, rubbing her palms over the silk folds of the wedding dress to settle her nerves. She was dressed in red, Ferrari red, as were Anwar and Tariq's children, who ran around her, sprinkling flowers and singing. They were perfect little flower children for their wedding. She pressed her palm over her swollen belly. Their unborn son kicked his presence, whispering from her womb, "I am here too."

Her heart filled with love and longing. Where was Fazza, and what was he up to? And then she saw the unmistakable convoy of Ferraris approaching. But who was driving? And then awareness dawned—the women who had come seeking empowerment whom she had taught to drive.

As the women began to gather, their faces beamed with excitement and nervousness. Grace couldn't help but feel a surge of pride. They came from all walks of life, each with a unique story. Some had escaped oppressive marriages, while others had bravely left behind traditional expectations. But today, they were all united by a shared desire for the freedom of unconditional love.

A fleet of gleaming Ferrari convertibles, generously provided by Fazza, had been gifted to each of the new drivers to celebrate Grace's and Fazza's wedding. The sight of these powerful machines, fuelled by the latest advances in solar power, juxtaposed against the backdrop of the palace filled Grace with awe. It was a symbol of the possibilities that lay before these women—the chance to take control of their own lives.

It was the perfect wedding, Grace mused as she approached each woman, offering encouragement and support. She saw the determination in their eyes and knew they were ready to embrace the challenge ahead and the freedom that awaited.

The engines roared to life, filling the air with a symphony of power and possibility. Tariq whispered in Grace's ear, sharing the joyful lap of victory he had planned. She climbed into a Ferrari convertible, festooned with orchids, leading the convoy as they embarked on their journey towards empowerment. With a wave of her hand, she signaled for the women to follow, and the cars set off, their sleek bodies gliding through the city streets.

As they cruised along the palm-lined boulevards, Grace could see the women growing increasingly confident with every passing minute. The wind whipped through their hair, a tangible reminder of the newfound freedom they were experiencing. Grace couldn't help but smile, knowing that she had played a small part in bringing about this transformation.

They navigated the busy streets with ease, their hesitations melting away as they realized the power they held in their hands. It was a moment of pure liberation, a testament to these women's strength and resilience.

As the convoy returned to the Palace, the women stepped out of the cars, their faces radiant with joy and accomplishment. They gathered around Grace and followed her down the flower-lined paths toward the beach, their eyes shimmering with gratitude.

As she stood beside Fazza, her husband-to-be, surrounded by her new family and the women whose lives she had empowered, she knew she had made the right decision. Fazza's love had provided them with a sanctuary, a home, and a country in which she could make a difference.

As the final wedding vows were uttered, she heard the words, "You may kiss the bride."

A question crested Fazza's brows as he gazed at her vibrant, matt-red lips.

"Ferrari Red is a kissable lipstick—able to endure the most passionate kiss," she affirmed.

Fazza bent his head toward her. 'Let's take Poppy's lipstick for a test drive," he murmured.

And the lipstick, like their love, proved a keeper.

EPILOGUE

"We shall name our son Hamza after your beloved grandfather," Grace said, cradling her newborn baby.

Fazza smiled. " I thought you would want our child to have a Western name inspired by the movie stars Tom Cruise, Brad Pitt, or George Clooney."

"Absolutely not!" she laughed.

"You do our son a great honor. My grandfather was a strong and beautiful man."

Was.

He forced his mind to his son, taking his tiny hand, savoring his newness, untainted by the past. "*Marhabaan, habibti*. Hello, my love," he said, staring into his large, innocent eyes.

Fazza didn't want to recall his grandfather's brutal murder. He would not dignify his assassin with that bloody memory. He would not permit the knowledge that his Grandfather's son, Fazza's father, had killed Hamza in his grab for power. He would not allow those painful memories to rob his son's future. Hamza, his grandfather's namesake, would have a different future, one Fazza vowed to protect.

"My grandfather always said, 'Teach your children to love,'" Fazza said, lifting his son from his mother's arms and cradling him in his arms.

Teach your children to love—the words Hamza had spoken to his son, Fazza's father, only to fall on blocked ears. Wasn't this why there was so much hate in the world? People had stopped listening to their hearts.

"Our son will love because he is loved deeply. He will make his grandfather proud. He will listen to his heart—as I have done," he said, placing a lingering kiss on Grace's lips.

"Families are meant to love," she said, knowing with certainty that her wounded past was now behind her. "Sometimes, there's nothing better than family."

Fazza's heart swelled. Their love had changed their lives. She had been a sister, a daughter, an aunt, and a cousin and had been callously abandoned by her family. Envy sought to destroy her, and love saved her. Now Grace had a new family—his family—the na Hassirs. And they loved her unconditionally. She was now a mother, a wife, a sister-in-law, and a princess. She would never feel alone or discarded again.

"Paradise," Fazza whispered, looking into Hamza's wide brown eyes. "It's what my grandfather strove to create. Loving families and heaven on earth. Let us do this together," he said impulsively as inspiration struck. Let us create a new city for our people—one not driven by commerce and endless shopping malls. But a town that embodies heaven in every way, where our people, the citizens that Hamza will one day rule, can flourish."

"Love," Grace murmured. A city where love rules. A city unlike any other in the world. A city that feels like a different planet. What a wonderful vision." She smiled and held out her hand.

"Love," Fazza agreed, drawing her hand to his lips.

"Lemuria," she said. "Do you remember what I told you about the ancient city?"

'Tell me again, *habibti*.'

"Lemuria was an ancient civilization where everyone lived in harmony, peace, and unconditional love for each other. There was no hatred, and no wars. It was a golden age filled with beauty, love, and light. Everyone lived in remarkable tranquility and innocence."

Innocence, he thought, gazing at his son. What a wonderful vision—a city where child-like innocence, untainted by adults' greed, ruled supreme.

As he gazed out at the sprawling palace, a fully rendered vision of the lost civilization idea began to take shape in his imagination. Inspired by the ancient world of Lemuria, Fazza envisioned creating a city that would transport its inhabitants to a bygone era.

In his vision, the city of Lemuria would rise from the desert sands, its majestic architecture reminiscent of ancient temples and palaces. Fazza imagined vibrant marketplaces filled with exotic spices and treasures, where the scent of incense and the sound of music would fill the air, just as they had in ancient days.

It would be unlike other cities he had built blazing with harsh neon lights and modern steel and glass structures encircled by motorways engineered for speed. No, his new city would embrace the mantra, 'slow.'

"The city will be adorned with lush gardens and flowing waterfalls, bringing life and serenity to the bustling streets. In the center of Lemuria, a grand palace will stand, its golden domes and intricate mosaics reflecting the glory of a forgotten era. It shall be a shrine to our love," he said, handing his son to Grace. "Of love for each other, our son, and our people's health and happiness."

Grace smiled. "A city where art, culture, and knowledge will thrive. With grand libraries filled with ancient texts and wisdom, where not just scholars can gather to exchange ideas and expand their understanding of the world, but all seekers of knowledge —regardless of gender, race or economic status."

"Yes. Yes," he said, clapping his hands in agreement. "In this city, education would be paramount, and schools would be built to nurture the minds of the young. It will be a place where the next generation will learn about the wonders of the ancient world, igniting their imaginations and fueling their curiosity."

"But what name shall we give our beautiful city of love and peace?"

"Ya Kalbi," Grace said instantly. *"My Heart."*

As the sun began to set, casting a golden orange glow over the palace, Sheikh Fazza saw the people of *Ya Kalbi* come alive. The streets would be filled with laughter and music as performers and artists shared their talents with the world. The city would become a beacon of creativity and inspiration.

But Fazza's and Grace's vision went beyond just a physical city. They imagined a community built on the principles of kindness, compassion, and inclusivity. Ya Kalbi would be a place where people from all walks of life would unite, celebrating their differences and embracing their shared humanity.

As he continued to envision this magnificent city, Sheikh Fazza knew that turning their dreams into reality would require immense effort and dedication. But he was determined to bring the ancient world of Ya Kalbi to life, creating a sanctuary where people could escape the pressures of modern life and immerse themselves in a world of magic and wonder.

With their unwavering vision and the support of his people, Grace and Fazza set out on a journey to make Ya Kalbi a reality. As the world watched in awe, the city of Ya Kalbi began to rise, a testament to the power of dreams and the limitless possibilities of the human spirit.

As their ambitious project neared completion, Fazza remembered what Grace had once said to him. "Money can't buy love," he told her, "but it can build a city of dreams."

"Yes," she said, winding her arms around his neck, "But it was love that created it."

And Fazza knew she was right. Even when his mind had denied it, his instincts had recognized the truth. Whatever the odds had been against them, as the universe conspired in their favor, fate drew them together, their souls recognizing each other in a love that transcended time and space. Destiny's hand painted their love story with strokes of serendipity, leading them towards a future where their souls would forever be intertwined.

THE END

ACKNOWLEDGMENTS

This love story, like my previous romance novels, could not have been written without the assistance of my team of passionate BETA and ARC readers.

Loreli Jessee, I so appreciated your encouraging words after reading the first three chapters and your wonderful review after reading the completed story! Thank you! I also want to express my gratitude to Wioletta and Linda for posting your reviews on Amazon (Bookbub and Goodreads), and to JoAnne, who is always such a great support. I truly appreciate you.

Sharon, your proof-reading and suggestions to add several dramatic scenes to the book were invaluable. I am grateful.

Obviously, responsibility for any mistakes or typographical errors that find their way into the finished book falls on my fingers, not theirs.

I am blessed with many friends who fill my life with love and laughter at critical junctures during writing, especially Heather, Cindy, Judy, and Jaime Rose. I also want to give a heartfelt thanks to the prison guards at Rimutaka and Aroha Women's Prison, who inspired me to write sheikh romances many years ago during my former life as a Leadership coach.

Finally, I wish to extend my deepest gratitude and love to my partner, Lawrence (Lorenzo) who inspired the plot with his love of the passion and beauty of his Ferrari F430, Frida. My debt to him is immeasurable, as is my love.

AFTERWORD

I hope you loved BOUGHT BY THE SHEIKH! I'd be so grateful if you could leave a quick review or star rating on Amazon or Goodreads.

DON'T MISS OTHER BOOKS IN THE SERIES!

Claimed by the Sheikh (Tariq and Melanie)
    https://www.molliemathews.com/claimed-by-the-sheikh/

Stolen By The Sheikh (Anwar and Lucy)
    https://www.molliemathews.com/stolen-by-the-sheikh/

Continuing reading for excerpts

JOIN THE CLUB

Never miss a new release or giveaway! Sign up for Mollie's newsletter to stay in the loop—and receive a free love story. Check out a full list of books and bio at www.molliemathews.com. Follow Mollie on Social Media as @Molliewritesromance (because she does) And if you loved this book, please take a moment to leave a review once you're done. Thank you!

EXCERPT STOLEN BY THE SHEIKH

CHAPTER ONE

Truth? Where did anyone even begin, Sheikh Anwar na Hassir questioned. In a world enamoured with lies, the truth seemed as impossible as the rarest sapphire in his Ceylonese mines to extract.

It begins with finding the woman who brought the curse of shame onto his family. Lucy Gaysford. Except she wasn't Lucy Gaysford any more, he growled, reading the shortened name emblazoned across the gallery window, signalling the solo exhibition by artist Lucy Ford. Anwar wrapped the gold New Zealand Merino scarf tighter around his neck, stealing himself to New York's wintery bite as he stood outside the Manhattan art gallery and glanced in.

She had been economical with the truth before. What other secrets was she now keeping?

Why had he come? In pursuit of truth and justice, he told himself, registering the kick of anticipation that trembled through his stomach as he caught a glimpse of his target. His eyes trailed her backless dress, revealing the sensuous curve of her spine as she wove through the crowd. A jolt of longing quivered through him.

Beauty, that's all, he cursed, forcing forbidden desire to a dull, barely perceivable tremor. Dammit. Why couldn't he shake the longing, the need—the pain of her betrayal?

Family honour, came the answer. To find the truth no matter the cost. He clenched his fist, bending his formidable will to his purpose. He would force from her the confession that her escape had invaded. He would silence the uneasy sense that he had been mistaken. That it was his beloved cousin who was the cause of so much hurt. That Hamad might've lied was untenable. Wasn't it better to accept the deceit of a Westerner, a woman with whom he had a short, passionate fling, rather than yield to the realisation that his own family had betrayed his love?

He paused before joining the intoxicated crowd inside, liquored up with complimentary drinks designed to adle their minds and open their wallets. He turned and glanced at the snow-lined streets festooned for the festive season. Thankfully, the gallery had not gone overboard with tawdry tinsel and garish, neon Christmas lights celebrating the birth of the Christian son his culture did not recognise but knew instead as God's prophet. Instead, as he redirected his attention indoors, he noticed with admiration that both unsettled and pleased him that the gallery was a shrine to love.

Love! He mused, noticing discomfort prickle his skin. What did he know of love? Oh yes—love of the inanimate. That was his refuge. Art, nature, his prized exotic orchids, and Zephyr, his loyal falcon, from whom he was rarely parted. These were the loves upon which he could rely.

He narrowed his formidable gaze in search of the woman he was here to make atone for the sin of her betrayal. He would extract her confession and then be done with Lucy, whatever her name was, forever.

. . .

AVAILABLE NOW—ebook, print, and audio. You'll find all the links and bonus videos on my website:

https://www.molliemathews.com/stolen-by-the-sheikh/

Claimed

By The Sheikh

MOLLIE
MATHEWS

I hope you enjoyed reading about Anwar's older brother
Sheikh Tariq na Hassir. If you did, you'll enjoy his love story.

Read on for a free excerpt of this full length romance, Claimed by The Sheikh — is available in ebook, audio, paperback and hardcopy

CHAPTER ONE

"Are you trying to kill her?" Tariq na Hassir, the formidable ruler of the Kingdom of Avana, seized the animal handler's arm, forcing him to release the rope laced around the baby giraffe's neck.

"She has suffered enough trauma." Tariq dismissed the man with a fierce scowl that struck fear into enemies.

A slither of panic crept into the young man's hushed apology. "I am sorry, your Excellency."

"Release the others from their cages," Tariq growled.

The man did not have to be asked twice. He knew from experience that the Sheikh's retribution for disobedience would be swift and merciless.

"You are safe from harm," Tariq said softly, stroking the baby giraffe's long neck with a gentleness that belied his strength.

"No one will ever hurt you again, Noor," he said softly, impulsively naming her as his fingertips swept through the calf's fur. He let his long, supple fingers linger a moment upon her tail. Thankfully, they had saved her in time, he thought as he reached for the reins, clenching his powerful hands around the soft leather.

The rage he had first felt on hearing about the ruthless murder of the newborn's mother still roared through him. Had she been executed to pay a tail dowry to the father of some money-mongering bride, he wondered? Or did some heinous person pay thousands of dollars for a wretched fly swatter?

Noor looked up and met Tariq's dark gaze. In her innocent eyes, he saw her despair, her disillusionment, her disgust with humanity. He recognized her trauma as though it was his own. Because it was.

"Humans," he said, his voice marinated with contempt. "The people you should be able to trust, the people who say they care, the people whose actions should be driven by love —the majority are driven by nothing but selfishness, deception, and lies."

Taking a bottle of milk, he placed the teat to Noor's lips. The calf's silky black lashes grazed her cheeks as she gazed down at the foreign object and then looked back at Tariq. She stared silently up at him, her eyes moist and bewildered.

Tariq had trained himself to shut down his emotions, but that skill suddenly failed him. His chest trembled with suppressed rage, knowing the orphaned baby would never again taste her mother's milk.

"What passes for love among some people is abhorrent," he said in a low, strained voice. "On behalf of humanity, I apologize."

The killing of the calf's mother and three other rare Kordofan giraffes by trophy hunters seeking their tails further motivated the Sheikh's commitment to transform his anger into action.

"Do you really think you can save her?"

Tariq looked at Anwar, his younger brother by 11 months.

His head was slightly bowed, but he could see his eyes were fixed in sadness and longing.

Tension ripped down Tariq's spine. "Our father's reign of terror and tyranny have robbed Avana of prosperity and peace. I will make it my personal mission to right the injustices of the past. War and hostility must end. And it starts with how we treat those most vulnerable."

His fingers shook as he gripped the bottle of milk as Noor, at last, began to suckle.

An eerie silence swept across the precipitous landscape of Avana's Tiwa oasis. Tariq lifted his gaze to the horizon. The only movement visible to his naked eye was the wind etching a delicate furrow as it crawled over the golden dunes.

"Not only will I provide a sanctuary for hunted wildlife and orphans like Noor, but I will liberate God's most precious creatures from the many closing zoos and other inhumane habitats around the world," he glanced over at the other animals being unloaded from the custom-built crates.

"I will create a world-acclaimed sanctuary, impenetrable by those with impure and malicious hearts. It will be the most magical, marvelous, mesmerizingly unique place, the number one eco-tourism destination in the world. I will create meaningful employment for our people, restoring their dignity, attracting millions of visitors annually, and contributing billions to the economy. But more importantly, I will show the world how kindness and compassion can be turned into plutonium and change the world."

Anwar glanced at the now lush landscape and recalled how barren it had once been. With no sign of life in sight, others had found it impossible to fathom his brother's vision to transform the punishing and unforgiving conditions into a haven for so many endangered species. Yet, as with everything Tariq turned his formidable will and mind-blowing wealth to, he had succeeded where mere mortals were destined to fail.

Anwar's heart swelled with pride as he thought of all his brother's achievements. "It's an audacious and admirable plan. And if anyone can pull it off, it's you, brother. Your passion, your drive, your unrelenting ambition, and your pursuit of goals exceed mere mortals. And you have the endurance and power of 13,000 Arabian horses, but aren't you setting yourself up for too much hard work? Why don't you relax? Kick back. Enjoy the fruits of your reign?" Anwar said, tossing his head in the direction of the harem. "Other men would."

"Women were our father's weakness," bitterness bled from his words. "I, too, once made the same mistake. I, too, paid the price."

There was a tense silence while Tariq lifted his gaze to the sky and studied the giant falcon circling above.

"Was it not you who once taught that your greatest weakness can also be your greatest strength?" Anwar asked.

Tariq shook his head, biting down a terse retort. "I was misled." He said, nodding his command to the animal handler lingering at a respectful distance.

He petted Noor as she was led away. "All kinds of atrocities are committed in the name of love, which is why it is the most dangerous of emotions and why I am forever turned off to women."

AVAILABLE NOW—ebook, print, and audio. You'll find all the links and bonus videos on my website:
https://www.molliemathews.com/claimed-by-the-sheikh/

. . .

If you enjoyed meeting lipstick designer Poppy Pac, you'll love her and Ethan's special love story in the full-length book *For The Love of Lipstick.*

Keep reading for a sneak peek.

Let passion provide the ultimate escape…
the *Montana Brides* series, where it's never too late to find love
Coming soon!

EXCERPT: FOR THE LOVE OF LIPSTICK

I f my own mother doesn't love me, who will?

44-year-old Poppy Pac sat alone in her dimly lit living room, surrounded by a sea of tissues and the lingering scent of sorrow. Her beloved husband, James, had passed away just a month ago, leaving behind an emptiness that seemed impossible to fill. As a mortgage broker, Poppy had always been the strong and capable one, guiding others through the complexities of homeownership. But now, she felt lost and adrift in a world that no longer made sense.

She had spent her life trying not to be noticed, deferring to her husband, who was content to write poetry, while she worked diligently in a shadow career, in part to avoid her mother's envy. But now James was gone—and her mother offered no comfort.

Her best friend, Lizzie, knew that Poppy needed something to pour her grief into, something that would ignite her passion and bring a glimmer of light back into her life.

. . .

The next afternoon, Lily arrived at Poppy's doorstep carrying a bag filled with an array of colorful pigments, waxes, and oils.

"Poppy," Lily said gently, her voice filled with empathy, "I know how much you loved making things. Remember when we used to spend hours crafting together? "Do you remember the fun we had brewing lip gloss on the kitchen stove and pouring it into bottle caps for sale at school? I know it was a long time ago; but I thought maybe, just maybe, pouring your grief into your hobby of making lipstick could help heal your heart."

Poppy looked up, her eyes red and puffy from countless tears. She reached for a tissue and dabbed at her eyes, contemplating Lily's suggestion. Making lipstick had always been a passion of hers—a creative outlet that allowed her to express herself in a unique and vibrant way. But since James's passing, she had abandoned her hobby, feeling as though there was no joy left in her life.

Lily gently placed the bag of lipstick-making supplies on the coffee table, her eyes filled with hope. "I brought every-thing you need to get started. Remember how much fun we had experimenting with different shades and textures? Maybe, just maybe, rediscovering that joy could bring a spark back into your world."

Poppy stared at the bag, her mind swirling with a mixture of longing and uncertainty. Could something as simple as making lipstick really help her heal? She glanced at Lily, her friend's unwavering support shining through her eyes.

Taking a deep breath, Poppy nodded. "Okay, Lily. Let's give it a try. Maybe it's time to pour my grief into something beautiful."

Lily's face lit up with a smile, and together, they opened the bag, revealing a treasure trove of colors and possibilities.

They cleared the coffee table, making space for their creative endeavor, and Poppy felt a flicker of excitement deep within her soul.

"Do you remember that crazy mixture we made, melting down all our leftover lipsticks? It was such a beautiful shade. I wish I still had it," Poppy said, pressing her fingers to her nude lips. "I called it "Happiness" because I always felt so wonderful when I wore it." Her thoughts drifted back to James. She'd be wearing *Happiness* when they first met.

"Maybe we can make it again," Lily said as they began carefully selecting pigments and mixing and blending them to create a palette of emotions.

Poppy didn't know if she would find happiness again, but she found solace in the rhythmic stirring of the blend, losing herself in the swirls of color that danced before her eyes. With each stroke of the spatula, she felt a small part of her grief being transformed into something tangible and beautiful.

As they added waxes and oils, the mixture took on a soft and velvety texture, much like the touch of James' hand on her cheek. Poppy closed her eyes, allowing the familiar scent of vanilla and lavender to envelop her senses. At that moment, she felt a deep connection to her husband, as if he was guiding her hands and whispering words of encouragement.

With Lily's guidance, Poppy poured the mixture into small lipstick molds, watching as the liquid transformed into solid pillars of color. As they waited for the lipsticks to set, they shared stories of James, their laughter mingling with tears of remembrance.

Finally, the lipsticks were ready, each one a unique reflection of Poppy's journey through grief. She carefully wrapped them in delicate tissue paper, feeling a renewed sense of purpose and a glimmer of hope.

Days turned into weeks, and Poppy found herself creating more and more lipsticks. Each one became a testament to her strength and resilience, a tiny vessel of healing that she could share with others. As she applied the lipstick to her own lips, she felt a sense of empowerment, a reminder that she could still find beauty in a world that had seemed so dark after James' death.

COMING SOON!

BY MOLLIE MATHEWS

THE SHEIKHS UNTAMED BRIDES

CLAIMED BY THE SHEIKH
STOLEN BY THE SHEIKH
BOUGHT BY THE SHEIKH
THE SHEIKHS UNTAMED BRIDES BOX SET BOOKS 1-2

GEMSTONE BILLIONAIRES

THE ITALIAN BILLIONAIRE'S CHRISTMAS BRIDE
THE ITALIAN BILLIONAIRE'S SCANDALOUS MARRIAGE
GEMSTONE BILLIONAIRES 2 BOOK-BUNDLE BOX SET
GEMSTONE BILLIONAIRES 3 BOOK-BUNDLE BOX SET

TRUE LOVE

BY MOLLIE MATHEWS

LOVE IN VENICE (3rd place winner Koru Award)
LOVE IN MEXICO
LOVE IN SICILY
LOVE IN MONTANA (Coming Soon)

PASSION DOWN UNDER SASSY SHORT STORIES

TWIST OF FATE
LOVE ME FOREVER
FOREVER AND ALWAYS
LOVE ME AS I AM
THE LIGHTKEEPER'S LOVER
FINDING A HUSBAND
LOVE ALL OF ME
CRAZY FOR YOU

PASSION DOWN UNDER 2 BOOK-BUNDLE BOX SET
(Books 1 & 2)
PASSION DOWN UNDER 3 BOOK-BUNDLE BOX SET
(Books 1, 2 & 3)
PASSION DOWN UNDER 6 BOOK-BUNDLE BOX SET

ABOUT THE AUTHOR

MOLLIE MATHEWS writes fun, sophisticated, passion-filled contemporary romance. She is known for her "sensual, beautiful, empowered stories enveloped in true romance" (5-star review). Her books have resonated with a global audience. She has been featured in magazines, television, and radio.

A former child and family therapist Mollie passionately believes in the power of romance to transform people's lives. She loves Mother Theresa's words, *"We are all pens in the hands of a writing God sending love letters to the world."*

Her stories are unashamedly positive, optimistic, and full of fun and passion.

She is a graduate of Victoria University in Wellington, New Zealand, and has given keynote speeches at romance writers' conventions and international seminars.

Mollie follows the sun, dividing her time between New Zealand and exotic locations—wherever she intends to set her next romance novel. She lives with her very own romantic hero, Lorenzo—tall, dark, terribly handsome, and fluent in Spanish!

Follow her on BookBub https://www.bookbub.com/authors/mollie-mathews and on her blog https://molliemathews.word press.com

and sign up for Mollie's newsletter at www.Molliemathews.com and receive her FREE gift.

Be inspired by Mollie on Instagram www.instagram.com/molliemathewsauthor

Follow Mollie on TikTok www.tiktok.com/@molliemathewsauthor

Join Mollie on Facebook at www.facebook.com/molliemathewsnz

Check out her inspiration board on Pinterest www. nz.pinterest.com/molliemathews/

ISBN eBook: 978-1-99-105317-6

ISBN print: 978-1-99-105319-0

ISBN print D2D: 978-1-99-105318-3

Cover Design: © Steven Novak

Published by

Blue Orchid Publishing New Zealand

Blue Orchid
PUBLISHING

Visit www.molliemathews.com to read more about all our books and to buy them. You will also find features, author interviews and news of author events, and you can sign up for e-newsletters so that you're always first to hear about our new releases.